# Tales of the Mongoose and Meerkat

## Vol I: Pursuit Without Asking

# Tales of the

# Mongoose and

# Meerkat

## Vol I: Pursuit Without Asking

By Jim Breyfogle

Illustrations by Dark Filly

Cirsova Publishing

©2020

First printing: 2020

ISBN: 978-1-949313-28-4

Cover: Anton Oxenuk
Interior Illustrations: DarkFilly
Layout, Design: Cirsova Publishing

"The Battlefield of Keres" originally published in *Cirsova Magazine of Heroic Fantasy and Science Fiction, Volume 1 #6,* 2017

"Brandy & Dye" originally published in *Cirsova Magazine of Heroic Fantasy and Science Fiction, Volume 1, #8,* 2018

"Sword of the Mongoose" originally published in *Cirsova Magazine of Heroic Fantasy and Science Fiction, Volume 1, #10,* 2018

"The Valley of Terzol" originally published in *Cirsova Magazine of Thrilling Adventure and Daring Suspense, Volume 2, #1,* 2019

"The Burning Fish" originally published in *Cirsova Magazine of Thrilling Adventure and Daring Suspense, Volume 2, #2,* 2019

*For Lynn,*

*who shouldn't have to share a dedication with anybody.*

# Table of Contents

# The Battlefield of Keres

*Two months after the fall of Alness ( not that Mangos cares. )*

It was, Mangos thought, the stupidest bet he had ever made. Not that it should surprise him; he had been winning all evening. Arm wrestling, bar bending, handstands, and a dozen other tests of strength and agility had seen him victorious—each victory bringing another tankard of ale. Small wonder his pride was high and judgment low.

Now he sat, head down, the morning sun angling through the inn's window to illuminate the table before him. His head hurt, his stomach wouldn't sit quietly, and worst of all—"I don't even know who Gorman is," he muttered to himself.

"He fought for the Duke of Endgras."

Mangos lifted his head. A young woman sat across and further down the long table, her back to the fire. Mangos savaged his memory, trying to remember her. Dark hair, torn clothes, yes, she had been playing dice last night – and winning.

"He's dead then?" he asked.

"It's hard to say anything for certain, where Keres is concerned, but I think it safe to assume he's dead." Her tone was dry, lightly mocking, as though this should be common knowledge.

Keres—that name *did* have meaning. The Duke of Endgras, Keres—he mulled the names and came up blank. He wasn't in the mood for ignorance. Glaring at the woman, he wondered if she was setting him up. What could a ragged, dirty, bruised little bit of a girl know?

The woman laughed softly, as if his frustration amused her. "What do you know of Gorman?" he challenged.

"You don't care about Gorman," she said. "You just need his helm."

"So tell me of his helm."

"A tough find," she said. "It would be easier if you just admitted defeat and paid for the tankard of ale."

"No," Mangos answered, not even needing to think about it. He would not give Thierry the satisfaction.

"Then listen," she said. "Gorman served the Duke of Endgras. He was stationed near the center during the battle of Keres, but sometime during the battle he was lost. Had his body been plundered, news of his helm would be known, but it's not." She leaned forward, her green eyes clear and piercing. "Gorman's helm remains in Keres."

"Keres, battlefield," Mangos said. "I can go there." Life, since he had left Arnelon, had been less adventurous than he expected. This might be fun.

The woman cocked her head, "I don't think you have a proper appreciation of Keres."

The door opened, and the adventurer Thierry came in, all scars and swagger. Spying Mangos he shouted, "Mangos! My friend! Do you have the helm? No?" He shook his head in mock sorrow. "The way you spoke last night, I felt sure you would have it already."

Mangos winced as Thierry's shout knifed through his head. "I'll get it," he growled.

"How long? I'm thirsty now!" Thierry roared with laughter. "Maybe you want a drink, too?"

The thought made Mangos queasy. "No."

"Good! Because there's no ale for you until you bring the helm of Gorman." He towered over Mangos as he said, more seriously, "Your tricks didn't impress me last night, and I'm not impressed now. You want to make a name for yourself—pfah!" He sauntered across the room and shouted for the barmaid.

Mangos ground his teeth, knowing Thierry shouted on purpose. Mangos knew he was stronger and faster, and Thierry chose this bet to embarrass him. He wished he had realized it last night. "I will not lose that easily."

He leaned toward the woman; he spoke low so Thierry couldn't hear, "Do you know where Keres is?"

She nodded.

He'd be damned if he let Thierry get the better of him, even if it meant asking this woman for help. "Will you help me?"

She didn't answer, just looked at him, sizing him up. Perhaps she was stupid or indecisive, but watching her face, he got the feeling she saw deeper into his question than he did. If she thought to rob him in the wilds, she would get a nasty surprise.

"Yes," she said finally. "I will help you."

"Good. What's your name?"

"Kat."

"How soon can you be ready to leave?"

"Gorman's helm hasn't moved in sixty years," Kat said. "I'll take a few minutes to clean up. One should look one's best when beginning a project."

Mangos sighed. "I'll wait outside."

He blinked when Kat joined him a short time later. She had washed her body and hair. He looked at her closely for the first time and realized she was pretty. No, he corrected himself, if you ignored the bruises and torn clothes, she was *beautiful*. It was like turning around and finding your sister all grown up.

His headache had subsided, and he felt foolish standing in the middle of the road, ready to drag this woman on his quest to find the helm of a fallen hero. Perhaps it was the ridiculously small stakes involved.

"If you give me directions, I can find it," he said.

Kat rearranged the small pack she carried. "If it were that easy, somebody else would have found it. We'll need to stop in Endgras. I want to search their archives." She started down the road.

With two long strides, Mangos caught up with her. "I'll make it up to you. I'll—"

"Give me half your winnings?"

Mangos felt his face turn red. "No, that wasn't what I meant. I'll..." he fumbled for words because he didn't know what would be fair payment. He gathered his dignity and said, "I am a great adventurer."

"If you were, you wouldn't need to say it," Kat said. "Although," she added before he could protest, "you showed good skill, if not judgment, last night."

Who was she to judge his skill? Mangos wondered. He had thought she might be an escaped slave, but she sounded too confident. A gladiatrix maybe?

He kept wondering as they travelled in easy silence. Kat looked completely comfortable. She kept a good pace and didn't stop or complain. She seemed content in her knowledge of him—which made him wonder if he had said things last night he couldn't remember. Maybe she was a good judge of character. Maybe she didn't care.

But he liked her company, and he was glad she was there, even if he knew so little about her.

After passing through a couple of small towns, Kat looked completely different than when he first met her. She bought new clothes, plain and sturdy, and other gear she lacked. He was surprised, given her apparent poverty, but she reminded him while he wagered ale, she only took money.

She bought a sword, as well—small, to suit her size, but the best available. Mangos prided himself on knowing his steel, and she clearly did too. But when he asked her where she learned it, where she came from, or who she was, Kat answered with long silences. Since he didn't want to risk his bet or her company, he didn't press. Instead, he asked of Keres, and she told him what she knew.

"You said Keres was big," Mangos said as he chewed on a duck leg. If it didn't have wings, Mangos might have thought this tavern served rats. He had entered Endgras hungry, and waiting while Kat stopped at the archives only made it worse. "But really, how big can a battlefield be?"

"You could ride two days east to west and not cross it," said Kat. "And it stretched from the Karris Mountains in the north to the Balmis swamp in the south." She looked up from her scroll. "That's fifty miles." More scrolls curled on the table beside her. An extra candle sat next to her, illuminating her face, the scroll, and the plate of fried duck that sat between them.

Mangos grunted, reluctantly impressed. "I'm surprised they let you take the scrolls."

Kat returned to reading. "They don't know I have them."

"Ah, that explains it." Mangos picked up his cup as he thought of the crumbling city surrounding them. At one time it was one of the largest cities on the eastern continent. Its lands had stretched far in every direction—rich, prosperous, and powerful.

Now it was a shell, its strength destroyed in the Keres, ruled by others while its eastern lands lay cursed by the battle. Of the tens of thousands who once lived here, only a few thousand remained; bone pickers, scavengers mostly, who sifted through the ruins of the city for old caches of wealth.

Mangos leaned over the table trying to see what she read. "What have you found?"

"Not much I didn't know," Kat admitted. "By the end of the first week of battle, things were so confused that nobody knew what was happening. The battle lines had long since broken down. Messengers disappeared." She shrugged.

"But it is known that Gorman was near the center."

"That's where he was when the battle started," Kat said.

Mangos didn't feel reassured. If they couldn't find Gorman, he would lose his bet. "We have time to look," he said.

"The Keres still claims victims."

The voice came right beside them, and Mangos jumped. Wine sloshed out of his cup. Without looking up, Kat swept her scrolls away just before the wine splashed them.

Mangos glared at the man who seemed to have appeared next to them. He looked...worn, if a person can look so. He had a long face, his mouth turning down in the corners. His skin and hair were pale. His clothes looked to be of better quality but faded. For a brief second, his lips turned up in what Mangos took to be an apology.

"Why do you say that?" Mangos asked.

"Adventurers go to the old battlefield looking for weapons, or armor, or magic. Often, all they find is death. They told me you visited the archives." He flicked his gaze around the table. "I see you took some of it with you. You're from the north," he said to Kat. "You're not," he told Mangos.

"Arnelon, I'm from Arnelon," Mangos said. He glanced at Kat. From the north? Maybe, she did have a little of the look.

Kat neither hid nor apologized for the documents. "Why did you seek us?"

The man bobbed his head around. "Boredom, maybe. Normally I take some small pleasure in the thought of grave robbers dying amongst those old perils. But you, my dear, are too pretty, and it sorrows me that you should perish."

She smiled. "Life is full of sorrow."

"True. Sadly true." He pressed his palms together and bowed his head. "But what do you seek on the field of Keres?"

"Gorman's helm," said Mangos wincing as Kat kicked him under the table, "would be nice to find," he added hastily. "But we're after Alazar's Crystal of Sight." Kat might have mentioned it sometime as they travelled. It sounded familiar.

"You won't find both together," said the man. "Alazar fought for Balmis at the north end of the field. Gorman, of course, held the center for Endgras, a dangerous position.

"Do you know," said the man, "artifact hunting is a very dangerous pursuit?" A kind of mad glitter came into his eyes as if the

13

idea excited him, though otherwise his expression did not change.

Mangos did not answer, and neither did Kat.

The man stood motionless. After a long silence, he said, "I buy antiquities and artifacts from Keres. I buy them all."

Kat lifted her head from her scroll. "All of them? Nobody else buys any?"

"Nobody else employs street urchins with sharp knives and stealthy ways."

Mangos set down his duck leg. He frowned, but before he could do more Kat said, "I'm not sure if we're being warned, threatened, or just talking."

"Words are words," said the man, "and not to be confused with knives in the dark."

Mangos tried to puzzle this out. "Who are you?" he asked.

"Forgive me. I am Karl, dealer of historic artifacts." He stopped talking, it seemed he had no more to say, but he stood looking at them.

Mangos waited for him to leave, but he remained standing. Finally, Mangos said, "Why don't you hunt artifacts for yourself?"

"We all hunt them in different ways."

Mangos had no answer and fell silent. Karl stood, watching.

Kat returned to reading.

Mangos picked up a piece of duck, toyed with it, held it up for Karl to see. "Want some?"

"Thank you, no."

"Well then, off you go." He made a shooing motion with his hands.

"Karl. Dealer of artifacts and curiosities. Do not forget." He seemed to glide from the room. "Anything I said," drifted back to them.

"An odd man," Mangos said.

Kat stared at the door. "Odd," she agreed after a moment.

"How far is it to Keres?" he asked.

"If we leave in the morning, we'll arrive early the next day. It would be best to spend as few nights on Keres as possible."

Mangos picked up the cold, greasy duck. "I'm not afraid." His gaze drifted to the door of the tavern. "And I'm not afraid of Karl."

"No," Kat said. "You shouldn't be afraid of Karl." Whether or not he should fear Keres, she left unsaid.

The road passed out of silent, crumbling Endgras city into the silent, desolate country. The fields were a jumble of brambles and stunted trees. Here and there, a homestead anchored a small farm. Grey clouds cast an ominous pall over the land, but it did not rain.

Stone pillars that rose waist-high marked their way. At first, Mangos thought them marking stones, but closer inspection revealed some still had rusted mountings and occasionally the remains of gears and chains attached to the top.

"A polybolos," said Kat, "protecting the supply lines and big enough to handle a dragon."

Mangos shook his head. "How do you know this?" He had never been one to worry about what he didn't know, but he couldn't help wondering again about her. Her knowledge was starting to scare him.

"It helps to know things."

He couldn't argue that.

"The Duke's command fortress is at the western edge of Keres," Kat said.

When they reached it the next morning, the fortress was unlike any Mangos had ever seen. It didn't look like a fortress, in spite of straddling the road. It had doors large enough to drive a cart through and windows to light the interior.

"Customs house," said Kat, and once she said it, he could tell. The road passed through a half-barrel tunnel, heavy gates rusting to nothing at either end. Rooms for confiscated goods crumbled to either side of the main building. "They used it as an administrative post when the war started."

Mangos walked to the nearest door and stuck his head inside. Night's cold still lingered within the building, and a bit of its darkness too. Once his eyes grew accustomed to the gloom, he could see it was empty except for rubble and a thick layer of dust.

Just as he turned to leave, some words caught his eye. Scratched into the wall by a manacle above a jumble of bones was "Madness saved me." Whether written by or written to mock the prisoner, Mangos could not tell.

Wind whispered through the building, stirring the cold air and raising bumps on Mangos's arms.

"This says what I've been trying to tell you," Kat called. Mangos found her in the tunnel, pointing to the wall. Graffiti covered the walls, words of men long dead. Time wore away the scratching, so little could be read from the soldiers who only once passed this way.

Kat pointed at some doggerel that survived:

*Should you venture past this gate,*
*Gird your weapon and hope forsake.*
*For Keres demands blood and gore,*
*And death shall feed it evermore.*

"Keres sounds like a beast, not a battle," said Mangos.

"Now," Kat said, "you're beginning to understand."

Walking to the end of the tunnel, Mangos looked out over Keres, trying to imagine what it must have been like during the battle. A seething mass of soldiers, fighting as far as you could see, punctuated by fire and magic, so different from the quiet, undulating land before him. It would have been mud and stone instead of grass and scrub brush.

"'Death shall feed it evermore.'" Mangos snorted. "Superstition."

"Which is undoubtedly what is still killing people."

"What do you think is killing people?"

"Traps, stray magic, restless spirits, unbanished demons," Kat said, "and artifact hunters."

"A carnival of death," Mangos said. He tried to laugh, but a shiver ran up his spine. "What happened to the Duke of Endgras?"

"He took the last of his men and rode into Keres."

"What? He didn't come back? Balmis didn't send his head home?"

Kat didn't answer, and Mangos didn't need one. Together they walked out of the tunnel and into Keres.

In spite of the sun, Mangos sometimes shivered, as if passing through pockets of cold air. The feelings came and went, and trying to discover the cause proved pointless.

They travelled east, searching amongst the quiet, grassy fields and ravines. Artifacts—helms, shields, and rotting timbers of war engines—littered their path. Sometimes, rarely, they passed a cairn, something that said in the midst of all the death somebody remembered their humanity and honored a fallen comrade. But these were invariably pulled apart, their contents plundered.

Noon came and went without any clue to Gorman's helm. They probed deeper, sometimes stopping to scrape the thin soil away from an oddity only to move on when it wasn't what they sought.

Later, Mangos saw the sun atop the rim of the ravine they climbed and noticed night gathered in the shadows below them. It would not be long before it crept out to cover the entire land. They should find a safe place to spend the night.

Movement caught his eye. "By the gods of Eastwarn, look at the size of that beast." A wolf, tall as a deer, stood on an outcropping.

"The wolves grew large on the dead," Kat said.

Mangos drew his sword. "We are not dinner." It may have been the wolf understood him, for it gave a growling bark. Another wolf appeared, slightly smaller than the first. More followed until seven huge wolves faced them.

"I'm not sure you should have mentioned dinner," Kat said.

Mangos swung his sword one-handed as he pulled out his dagger. "Come, beast, we'll see who's dinner."

One of the smaller wolves darted in, head down, and snapped at his leg. Mangos slashed its head, but its thick skull turned his blade. The wolf retreated, bone visible atop its grey head and blood pouring through its fur.

Two more dashed in, one from each side. Mangos thrust at one, while Kat lunged forward to stab the other. The rest of the pack swarmed over them, snarling and biting. Mangos buried his dagger hilt deep into one, but its body still knocked him over and tore the weapon from his hand. He gripped his sword with both hands and rolled back and forth, trying to avoid snapping teeth.

Next to him Kat curled, the wolf on her back all grey fur and gnashing teeth. He caught intermittent glimpses of her as she shook off the wolf and thrust, driving her sword straight into the wolf's mouth and out the back of its neck. She slashed another wolf's hind legs, making it collapse with a yelp.

Teeth and tongue filled his vision. He raised his sword—the wolf was too close to thrust or swing; he turned his weapon so the wolf bit down on the edges. It worried the blade, tearing itself badly before releasing the sword and backing away.

Mangos stood, glanced around. Kat stood next to him, resolute. Two wolves lay dead. Four others bled. The pack leader stood on the outcropping, watching.

"Care to go again?" Mangos asked.

The pack leader lowered its ears and bared its teeth, but gave a sharp bark. One of the wounded barked back, and the leader growled. The wounded wolf gave a little whine.

A chorus of tiny yips and howls burst from the cluster of rocks

where the wolf had first appeared. A litter of pups followed, tumbling over each other. The wounded gathered around them, guided them up the ravine, nipping and growling to keep the pups moving. The pack leader snarled, pacing until the rest were gone, then vanished after them.

"How's your back?" Mangos asked.

"Fine," said Kat. "I think it just tore my jacket." Mangos looked, nodded.

"That went—surprisingly well," he said. "You—" He stopped himself from saying, "didn't do anything stupid," and substituted, "fought very well." They *had* fought well together.

"Thank you," she said.

"Let's find someplace to rest that doesn't have wolves," he said. "And we can look for Gorman's helm in the morning."

By the time Mangos reached the ridge, the sun had just dropped below the horizon. It lit the western sky, but to the north, another glow, previously drowned by the sunlight, backlit a higher ridge.

Mangos pointed it out to Kat. "Maybe it's a conference of spooks."

She snorted her disbelief. "I wonder what it is."

He grinned. "Let's find out."

Except for the strange glow, it was fully dark when Kat led the way to the top of the ridge.

"What is it?" Mangos said as he hurried to catch up.

"Not spooks," she said.

Several miles away, a column of fire rose to the sky. Flames spiraled up to where the clouds took an orange glow.

"A tornado of fire," Mangos said. "A firenado, but it isn't moving."

"Unbelievable." Awe tinged Kat's voice. She shook her head slowly. "The records didn't mention *that*."

Mangos nodded. "Most magic is tricks and sleight of hand. This is incredible."

"Dicing is sleight of hand," Kat corrected him. "Magic is something else entirely."

"That should keep the wolves away," he said. "Let's go warm our hands."

It took longer than Mangos expected to climb the series of ridges and trudge through the valleys. Finally, the firenado glowed above the last ridge, and he heard its crackling roar. The air grew dry.

Mangos wiped his brow, drew a deep breath. Kat caught his eye, smiled and pressed ahead.

"It'll keep the wolves away, I'll grant you that," she said.

The heat hit Mangos as he climbed onto the ridge, making it difficult to breathe. Wind rushed past him, drying his sweat, but not cooling him.

The firenado roared on the opposite ridge and bathed the whole valley in orange light. The ground reflected the glow back. Hundreds, maybe thousands of bodies still lay where they fell, mummified. Their armor had been burnished by the heat and wind. Nothing grew, for the firenado carried away all the dust, leaving only stone and hard, baked earth.

Mangos licked his lips. "If the helm is down there, I'll for sure need a drink."

Kat drew her hair back. "I don't—" her voice cracked. She swallowed. "I don't think it is. The center is further south."

Mangos shaded his eyes. "What does it burn?"

"Nothing, it's magic."

"It must burn something."

"That is a major magical disaster," she said, still staring at the firenado. "An accident." She paused. "Maybe not an accident, but magic done beyond the boundary of control."

"It must burn something," Mangos insisted. "Ah! It must draw its fire from another dimension. Somewhere in another universe is a whirling vortex of cold."

Kat looked at him, something like surprise on her face. He couldn't tell if she thought him brilliant or ridiculous. "Perhaps," she said thoughtfully. She turned to leave, but Mangos stayed.

"There!" said Mangos, the word scratching his dry throat as it came out. A pile of bodies lay near the bottom of the valley. Men had died by the dozen there, and that meant a hero. "That mound of bodies—who is that?"

Kat came back beside him. "We're too far north," she said. "It can't be Gorman."

"How can you be sure? I'm going to look."

Kat did not answer, nor did she follow. She stood, her face orange from the firenado as he turned to investigate the bodies.

The wind pushed him forward. The heat radiated so strongly he thought he could feel his skin redden. He stepped, with exaggerated care, over desiccated corpses. Everything he did slowly, deliberately.

He thought he heard words, but over the wind and the dull roar of the firenado, he couldn't be certain. It didn't matter anyway, he told himself, for the mound of bodies was ... still far away. He didn't know if he should trust his eyes, for the hot air might distort distances.

He stumbled, and a few steps later stumbled again. The body in front of him grinned through shriveled lips. Its eyes had been vaporized. Mangos wondered if enemies had killed the man. Or had the firenado?

He blinked, and his eyelids scraped across his eyes like sandpaper. He couldn't think clearly. Why was he here? How had he come to be kneeling next to a dead man? What was Kat saying?

Kat's hair whipped past her, and she held up a fold of her cloak as protection against the heat. Mangos wanted to say something, but as he opened his mouth she lifted her other hand and squirted water from her flask. It went into his mouth and over his face, stinging his eyes.

She yanked him up, dragging him toward the ridge, only pausing to give him more water. He stumbled often, his legs weak, but she did not let him fall. Once at the top, she threw herself down the other side, protected from the heat and wind.

Mangos collapsed next to her and drank deeply of both cooler air and water.

"That's," said Kat, her words spaced by deep breaths, "not Gorman."

Mangos nodded and closed his eyes. He could almost feel them absorbing moisture. "Good."

For two days they worked their way south and east. Mangos complained of troubled dreams, the feeling of other beings crowding into his head at night. Kat admitted having the same feeling.

During the day, Mangos often saw things at the edge of his vision, but they vanished when he turned his head. He did not mention them because he didn't want Kat to think him foolish. They saw and avoided many hazards but did not find Gorman's helm.

"Here," said Mangos. "We must be near the center. This is where Gorman would be."

The ground was flat but riven with cracks. At places they could see hints of the old road, at one point even the foundations of a bridge, but only grass grew for miles around.

In spite of being flat, the ground was lumpy and uneven, treacherous to walk on. When Mangos rubbed his foot across the grass, it pulled away. The soil was thin over a rusted breastplate. He took a step and felt something crunch as he put his weight down. Armor or bones, he could not tell.

"Heroes do not die common deaths," said Kat. "Look for something more than this."

Mangos nodded, walking forward, sometimes slipping when the grass slid off an old skull, sometimes crunching through rusted armor or weakened ribs. He stepped on someone everywhere he placed his feet.

"Who's that?" Kat said.

Mangos looked up in time to see two men, unnoticed earlier, disappear in a crevasse.

"Thierry!" said Mangos. "He wants to claim the helm before us! The scoundrel! He's too cheap to buy drinks, so he has to steal our treasure!" Mangos began to run, not minding his footing. He heard Kat's light footsteps behind him.

Mangos reached a valley, somewhat deep, rather short, but well lit by the overhead sun. Thierry picked his way down the wall, his face obscured by a large shield strapped to his back. He was half way down, his companion followed.

"Stop, you thief!" shouted Mangos, only to be answered by laughter.

"Look!" said Kat. She pointed to the far side of the valley. "Gorman!"

A body in white armor lay under an overhang. It lay as though placed there, on its back, gauntleted hands folded over its chest, helm placed carefully next to its head.

"You thief!" shouted Mangos as he threw himself down the wall, scrambling to catch up with his former drinking companion. He took chances and moved quickly, but it was apparent Thierry had too much of a lead.

Thierry reached the valley floor. "You should be buying the drinks for me!" he called up.

"That wasn't the bet! We bet whether *I* could return with Gorman's Helm!"

"Well, you can't because the helm is mine," Thierry shouted.

"A cheater and a thief!" Mangos barely noticed the small cuts on his hands from the rocks as he hurried to catch up.

Thierry reached Gorman's body just as his henchman and Mangos both reached the valley floor. Only then did they all notice the creature, an imp really, who sat behind Gorman.

It had dark red, mottled skin, short but wicked horns curling from its head, and claws that shone ivory on one hand. As it climbed over the body they noticed the other arm was truncated above the wrist, and scars crisscrossed its muscular body. It stood less than waist high.

Thierry laughed, and his thoughts were clear. It might have been threatening if it weren't so...*small*. The imp regarded Thierry warily as he approached, but did not run. Suddenly, Thierry swung his fist, catching the imp squarely and lifting it, slamming it into a boulder. It landed, lifted itself on its hand and stump, and shook its head slowly.

Thierry reached for the helm.

"No!" shouted Mangos. He leapt over a stone and charged Thierry. Thierry spun, shrugged his shield over his shoulder and drew his sword. He swung as Mangos neared.

Mangos drew in his breath, felt the sword tear the air in front of him. He drew his own sword.

Thierry attacked again, shouting for his companion. Mangos parried.

Mangos swung, but Thierry lifted his shield in time. "You're a fool," said Thierry. "Lucky to get this far."

"I," said Mangos, "will be the greatest swordsman the world has ever known."

"Oh, stop boasting," said Thierry as he turned aside another slash.

Steel clashed on steel behind him, but Mangos didn't turn. The sound did not stop, but continued rhythmically, with Mangos's attacks adding dissonant sounds.

Thierry sucked in his breath. "You'll never even be as good as *she* is."

With a twist of his wrist, Mangos caught Thierry's sword with his own and slid it down to bind in his cross-guard. He yanked, pulling Thierry forward. With another twist he bent Thierry's sword and freed his own, swung up, catching Thierry's shield and throwing it upwards. He swung under the upraised shield, cutting through Thierry's side, cleaving his gut, and out near his far hip.

Thierry straightened, but his torso kept falling back while his legs stayed in place. His guts cascaded out onto the ground before he fell over entirely.

Mangos turned to check on Kat. She sat on one of the rocks, legs crossed, elbow on one knee, head on her hand, looking bored. Thierry's henchman lay face down and clearly dead.

"That dratted thief!" Mangos said. "Now there's no one to buy my drinks."

The imp had crept back in front of Gorman. It hissed and stood a little straighter as Mangos approached.

"Step aside, little beast," Mangos said.

"He's guarding it," Kat said.

"Surely he is, and he can guard all but the helm when we leave."

"Suit yourself, but I'd leave it there."

Mangos laughed. "After coming all this way? Who would believe us if we didn't have the helm?" He stretched out his hand.

The little imp hissed, sounding like a cat, and took a deep breath. It expanded, kept expanding, growing taller and wider; skin stretched taut over massive muscles. It had teeth like knives, claws like scimitars. Sparks crackled between its horns, and a tongue of fire licked from its mouth. No longer an imp, a demon towered above them. Now it sounded like the roaring of a lion.

"Hey!" Mangos shouted as he jumped back.

With its one hand, the demon picked up a large rock. It held up the rock and crumbled it like a piece of dry cheese.

"I can take strong," Mangos said.

The demon blew fire just far enough to make Mangos move back.

"Hey, that's not fair!" he exclaimed. The heat reminded him of the firenado, and his mouth went suddenly dry.

"That," said Kat, "is a good reason to leave the helm behind." The demon rumbled agreement. "It's guarding Gorman," Kat continued. "It won't bother you if you don't touch the helm."

"Not the helm," Mangos said. "Maybe the gauntlets?"

The demon held up its hand and snapped his claws together.

"Not the gauntlets either." He sighed. He brightened up with a thought. "Well, Thierry wasn't going to buy drinks anyway." He sheathed his sword and backed further away.

As Mangos backed away, the demon seemed to relax. It tore off Thierry's head, tossed it into the air and caught it in its mouth on the way down.

Mangos turned away and started to climb out of the valley, trying to ignore the rending and crunching sounds. He felt very good about not taking the helm.

"You knew it could transform," he said.

25

"I would stay to ask how the demon got here," Kat said, not admitting anything as she climbed next to him, "but I don't want to disturb its lunch." The crunching sounds began again. She smiled. "You can't win every bet."

"No point going back now. Thierry is dead, and I didn't get the helm."

"There's always treasure," Kat said. "Always adventure."

"We didn't even get the helm," he repeated.

"Our first time," she said. "We'll get better."

He paused, thought of the travel, the danger, and the lure of treasure. "Did you have anything in mind?"

"A jewel that was lost?" She laughed, shook her head. "Why ruin the pursuit with the goal? Sooner or later, we all come to the treasure we most covet."

Mangos grinned. "Then let us pursue without asking what we chase, and when we catch it, let us chase again!"

# Brandy and Dye

*Four months after the fall of Alness.*

**M**angos watched the birds fly below him, their rich, dark red feathers in contrast to the white tops of the clouds. The sun shone through the hole in the mountain, illuminating birds and clouds even as it left the rest of Talhorn Mountain in shadow.

The hole couldn't possibly be natural, but there was no reason for god or man to carve a perfect circle five hundred feet across clear through the mountain. It existed as a mystery, sitting at the valley's head, but because it was on the edges of the world, nobody cared.

The plank deck of the rope bridge swayed as Kat came up behind Mangos. She paused to look over the edge. "Minix bird," she said. "That's what it's all about."

The clouds gave the illusion that the valley was only a hundred yards deep and dusted in cotton. In truth, only the makeshift bridge deck and rope handrails kept them from falling seven thousand feet to the valley floor.

"You'll not want to fall," a man said. He stood on the edge of a *holmen*, one of the spires of rock that rose from the valley floor. The network of rope bridges connected the numerous *holmen* with each other and the ridge that divided the valley in two.

"I didn't think I did," Mangos muttered as he finished crossing. "Are you Harlin?"

"If you're the two adventurers I'm expecting, then I'm Harlin." He snorted loudly, dragging phlegm from his throat and spitting it over the edge of the *holmen*.

"Mangos," Mangos said. "My partner Kat." He half turned so Harlin could see past him as Kat crossed the bridge.

Harlin scratched white dust from his hair as he peered at Kat. "You're pretty. You remind me of my sister. Except she wasn't pretty."

Mangos wasn't sure of the compliment, but Kat acted as though she expected it. She should, Mangos thought, for men always acknowledged her beauty but never showed any desire. He didn't ask why, though he sometimes wondered.

"You sent out a call?" Mangos asked. A call for adventurers with an offer of a royal reward. He liked the sound of that.

"You know what we do here?" Harlin asked.

"You mine Minix guano and process it to make dye," Kat said.

Harlin nodded. "Exactly. The birds eat the ridge berries." He pointed to the ridge dividing the valley, which was green with bushes. More bushes grew atop the *holmen*. Mangos could see red berries on the nearest ones.

"They eat the berries, and they," he looked at Kat and clearly changed the word he was going to say, "poop. We make the poop into dye."

"People want bird *poop* dye?" Mangos asked.

"The dye never fades," Harlin said. "It smooths the fibers of the cloth, making wool feel like cotton, cotton feel like silk, and silk feel like heaven."

"No accounting for what people will do," Mangos said.

"The color is absolutely unique, and the dye very rare," Kat said. "Only kings and emperors were allowed to wear it during the Age of Empires. That's why it's called Royal Dye."

"We make so little that we can't even fill the demand of the kings and princes of today," said Harlin.

"So what's the trouble?" Mangos asked.

"Distillers. They harvest too many ridge berries to make their brandy. The birds don't have enough. The birds eat less, we have less—" he hesitated as he substituted again, "guano."

"Can they eat anything else?" Kat asked.

"No. If the Minix birds eat anything except ridge berries, their guano won't make good dye."

"Huh," mused Mangos, glancing at the green ridge, down at the carpet of clouds hiding the valley floor, and at the spidery network of bridges the workers must cross.

"They've hired thugs to intimidate my workers," Harlin continued. He stuck a grimy finger up his nose and fished around until he was satisfied. He inspected the result and flipped it over the rail. "The guano dust gets into you," he explained. "Into your eyes and nose, and folds of your skin."

"Lovely," Kat murmured.

"You need to stop the distillers. Dyers have been harvesting guano from these *holmen* for generations. Now these distillers are destroying our trade. I don't care what you do," he raised his eyebrows, clearly conveying any option, no matter how gruesome, was acceptable, "but get it done."

The next morning, the sun crested the eastern horizon, flooding the valley with light and making the clouds glow gold. The Minix birds flitted around the ridge, dots of motion rising from and settling back into the green bushes. Smaller flocks ate from the bushes growing on the *holmen*.

The scrapers were already up, putting on their harnesses and tying to the safety pins. They tied their buckets to their belts and held their tools through loops of cord.

The clouds parted enough to see down to the valley floor. Mangos then realized how ridiculously thin the *holmen* were, and wondered that they did not snap from the wind and their own weight.

"Don't drop your shovel," remarked Mangos to a nearby scraper. "That's a long way down."

The scraper shook his head. "Can't get it. Wind'll kill you," he pointed to the hole in the mountain. "The Devil's Arse funnels the wind coming through it down into the valley. We're above it, but below the clouds, it'll take the flesh off your bones."

"Devil's Arse?" Mangos chuckled at the thought, looking at the hole more closely. With the sun lighting the face of the mountain, he could see the difference between the mountain rock and a massive ice ledge above the tunnel.

"You should see the snow swirl around in the winter," the man said. "The wind through the hole blows it back up until it catches on the mountain above or gets pushed to the side." He tugged on his rope, nodded to Mangos, and began to lower himself off the side of the *holmen*.

"That explains why they work up here," said Kat, "and not down below."

Mangos nodded, looking down at the barren valley until the clouds closed back up. "The wind must be terrible indeed.

"Do you think the distillers will intimidate easily?" Mangos inquired as he ducked back into the small hut where they had spent the night.

"No." Kat started to gather her things.

Mangos shrugged. It didn't seem hard to run off some distillers. Just drop one over the edge and the others would see reason. "Where are they?"

"Over by the edge of the valley. There's a small grouping of *holmen* close to the north wall off to the east."

"We can just cut the bridges."

"You do that and I'll not pay you a thing," said Harlin. Mangos started and spun, only relaxing as he recognized the head dyer. "You've no idea how hard it is to string the first lines of a new bridge."

"Might be worth giving up a few *holmen*," Kat said.

"No. I want every square inch of ridgetop and *holmen* for growing ridge berries. I'm not giving up a thing. Those are the terms. If you don't like them, that's too bad."

His tone bothered Mangos. "It'd be easier—"

"I can cut the bridges myself," Harlin snapped. "I'm hiring you because I don't want to."

Mangos nodded, not trusting himself to speak. He grabbed his pack, knocking over a pile of supplies at the same time.

"Ha," Harlin gave a short barking laugh. He kicked a small keg that had been hidden by the pile. "Alcohol. Not supposed to be up here."

"Brandy?" Kat asked.

"No. Just raw alcohol we use in dye making."

Mangos eyed the keg. It would fit in his pack.

Kat smirked. "Seems like a drunk man would be susceptible to flying lessons."

Harlin laughed. "It happens. That's why I don't allow alcohol up here." He shrugged. "Glad to see you're getting on with the job."

"I guess he didn't mean he doesn't care what we do," Mangos said once Harlin left.

"He doesn't care what we do to the vintners." Kat said, "as long as it doesn't affect him."

When Kat looked the other way, Mangos pushed the keg into his pack. Harlin would assume whoever hid it came back, and the person who did hide it couldn't complain because it shouldn't have been there in the first place.

He braced himself and swung his pack over his shoulder, trying to make it look no heavier than usual. "Ready."

The distillers and dyers were essentially a small group of men sharing the same dangers so it didn't surprise Mangos they were expected. Two men stood at the far end of the bridge to the distillers' *holmen*.

"You've no business here!" one called.

Mangos slipped off his pack and walked onto the bridge. He felt it bounce as he crossed. "We do." A small stone slipped between the planks and dwindled to invisible as it fell.

The man who spoke stepped onto the bridge, unhooking a heavy club from his belt. "No, you don't. I'll drive it into your head so you'll remember." The second man carried an iron-tipped spear. A third appeared from a small tent on the *holmen*. He carried a crossbow and immediately fitted a bolt into it then began to work the crank.

"Not afraid of heights, are you?" asked the first man.

"No," replied Mangos, unconcerned by the swaying bridge or the long fall beneath him. He drew his sword. If this was how things were done here, that was fine, though the crossbowman worried him.

The man swung the club back and forth as he walked forward, timing his swing and steps so Mangos had to parry or give ground.

"Keep running," the man taunted. "It's the smartest thing you can do." The second man peered around the first, not interfering with his attack.

"You boys need to stop messing with the dye makers," Mangos said, stopping his retreat.

"Not your business," the man said then attacked.

Mangos spun, lay back onto the rope handrail, and let the club swing in front of him. The rope creaked with his weight, and he knew if it broke or his feet slipped he had a very, very long fall, and the last thing that would go through his mind would be his ankles.

His weight shifted the bridge, pushing it away from him and tipping it sideways. The handrail now supported his weight while his body forced the bridge deck to a steep angle.

Kat cried out but grabbed the other rail and leaned into the tilt, somehow keeping her feet.

The man with the club cursed as his feet slipped, he fell, then slid over the edge. The clouds, which looked so thick, did not stop his fall. He plunged inside and was lost from sight.

The spear wielder fell, grabbing the planks as his legs swung toward the abyss.

Mangos's feet slipped from the bridge. He clutched the rail, felt it dip again. The bridge swung back and struck him in the stomach, knocking the wind from him. His right hand slipped; he wrapped his arm around the rope and gripped it tight. Now he hung from the rope handrail, dangling past the deck of the bridge, gasping for air.

Kat advanced past him, not heeding the bridge's movement. The

last guard scrambled to his feet, trying to free his spear, which had stuck between two planks. He yanked it up just in time to fend off Kat.

"Get up," Kat ordered.

Mangos rolled his eyes, afraid to let go of the rope to grab the bridge. His heart pounded, and he found it hard to breathe.

"You killed Jarin!" the guard yelled, his eyes wide.

"It's a long way down," Kat said. "He's not dead yet." She turned her head so Mangos could see her profile. "Get up!"

Mangos heaved his legs up, doing no more than kicking the underside of the bridge. He tried again, managing to get one leg onto the bridge. He lay, mostly over air, one arm entangled on the railing, looking down.

The bridge rocked and swayed as Kat and the guard fought.

Letting go with his left hand, Mangos grabbed the bridge and pulled himself over, the railing rope rising as the bridge took more of his weight. As he stood nearly upright, he unwrapped his other arm.

"I dropped my sword," he said.

Kat glanced back. "Now we can kill this guy." She lunged, knocking aside the guard's spear and laying open his arm. She dropped her blade low, drew it across his leg, and stepped forward to shoulder him off the bridge.

He threw his spear so he could grab the railing. Kat plucked the spear from the air and threw it to Mangos. Then she cut the guard's hands from the rail, sending him screaming down to the valley.

"Well, doesn't this make all kinds of problems," the man with the crossbow said. He pointed the crossbow at Mangos. "I can kill you," he assured them.

"But you can't crank that thing fast enough to prevent me from killing you," Kat said.

"I could kill you instead."

"And face the same fate from me," Mangos added.

"The moment you pull that trigger you're a dead man," Kat said.

"Who joins me?"

"You don't have to die," Mangos said. "Stop harvesting berries, and there isn't a problem."

The man sneered. "Except how I would make a living. Besides, the problem really isn't my picking berries."

"Truce?" asked Kat.

"For how long?"

33

Kat brushed her hair back. "Until we can get close enough to kill you?"

The man snorted. "Two hours."

"Fine."

The man lowered the crossbow. Kat sheathed her sword. After a moment Mangos grounded his spear. "I'm not giving up on this job," he whispered.

"Of course not," whispered Kat. "But he thinks he's safe from us in two hours. I want to know why." She crossed over to the *holmen* and said, "If your picking the berries isn't the problem, what is?"

"Lijas," the man introduced himself. He didn't answer Kat's question, instead saying, "I started in the dye business. I made the grain alcohol that's added to the dye to keep it liquid. They don't need much, three gallons or so a year. The lads drink a lot, but not enough to keep me busy."

"And what does this have to do with our problem?" Mangos asked.

"I began experimenting with the ridge berries. I fermented them, which made a fair wine. Then I distilled it, which made a better brandy. Then I accidentally allowed the brandy to freeze, which serves to distill it again, and something happened. Fire in the first distillation, ice in the second, and the result is incredible. I cut it with meltwater from Talhorn and call it Imperial Brandy. I can set my price."

"And you're making too much," Mangos said. "The birds don't have enough berries to eat."

Lijas shook his head. "Here's the thing. Harlin's dye can only be made from Minix bird guano after the bird has eaten ridge berries. No berries, no guano. But, the berries only grow in soil fertilized by the guano. No guano, no berries. They have taken so much guano from the ridge and *holmen* that the bushes are sickly and don't produce much fruit."

"So you're saying it's not your fault."

"It's not. When Harlin took over from his father several years ago, he almost doubled his dye production. Now the bushes won't even grow on half the *holmen* anymore because the soil is too thin."

It made sense, and Mangos believed him. It meant stopping Lijas wouldn't solve Harlin's problem, but sometimes the world worked that way. There were no right or wrong sides of issues, only the side you were on.

"That doesn't change the fact that your making brandy means

34

fewer berries for the birds to eat," Kat said.

Lijas nodded. "Essentially, yes. But in another five years, there won't be any Ridge Berry bushes, so I don't see how it matters."

Thousands of Minix birds rose squawking from the ridge as workers crossed the bridges to begin scraping guano.

Lijas shook his head. "Stupid. They scare the birds off the ridge and *holmen*, so the guano falls into the valley. They should wait until afternoon, when the birds are done feeding."

Mangos ran his hand through his hair. "Doesn't some of the guano always fall in the valley?"

"Of course, but do you know how much guano it takes to make even one flask of dye? No, you obviously don't. I use in a season fewer berries than it takes to make the guano they waste by harvesting in the morning."

Mangos struggled to sort this out.

Kat shuffled her feet a little, moving the soil as if to see how thin it was. "Haven't you talked to Harlin?"

"Haven't *you* talked to Harlin?" Lijas countered. "You know how productive that is. It got me nothing, and I had to hire Jarin and Charl when somebody set fire to my still."

Mangos knew exactly who the "somebody" was.

"Huh," Kat said, clearly thinking. "It's our job to shut you down."

"Walk away," Lijas said. "You can kill me once the truce is up, but it'll kill you. Walk away now, and you might live."

"Ha! You think you can kill us?" Mangos thumped the spear on the ground.

Lijas set down his crossbow. "I don't need to. Those lads you killed were kin to half the workers up here, and friends to most of the rest. You'll have a dozen men after you as soon as word gets out. Stay around until our truce ends and you'll never make it off the *holmen*."

"Their kin must work for Harlin then," said Mangos. Why would family members work for bitter rivals, especially ones fighting each other?

"'Course. That's the reason I hired them. They'd not kill their kin, and their kin wouldn't kill them. Everybody makes the right noises and nothing changes. That suits me even if it doesn't suit Harlin."

"But they tried to kill us," Mangos pointed out.

Lijas smiled, looking a little sad. "I didn't say they were smart."

"And that's why Harlin hired people from outside the valley," Kat said. "Because he wanted change."

Lijas pointed to the other *holmen.* "Looks like word is getting out. The mob might be here before the truce ends. I'll warn you Jarin's brother is rash enough to cut bridges and Harlin be damned."

Mangos took a step toward the bridge. "I'd rather not be trapped on a *holmen.*"

Kat nodded. She stepped close to Lijas. "I'll not break the truce, but neither will I walk away from a job. We're not done here." She spun and led the way across the bridge.

Mangos followed, watching the men gathering on other *holmen,* mapping ways along the network of bridges, trying to figure a path to the valley's side.

There were two bridges to the valley side, one to the west, closer to Talhorn mountain, the other further east. They wanted the eastern one.

"We can take them," Mangos said as he picked up his pack.

Kat glanced over her shoulder. "Unless they cut the bridges."

"There is that," Mangos frowned.

"Or they have bows."

"That too."

The sound of pounding footsteps and creaking ropes surrounded Mangos as he and Kat raced from *holmen* to *holmen.* Workers shouted the news to other workers, who pulled themselves up like insects to the tops of the *holmen.*

The men gathered in twos and threes before moving together to form larger groups. They brandished pickaxes and iron bars, and a couple had small bird bows.

"Go east," Mangos said. Any fight would slow them until they could be overwhelmed. He began to run.

"Cut them off!" Four men ran toward the eastern bridge. "Stop them from escaping!"

"West!" called Mangos, as their escape east was blocked. They veered off, seeking a way around, but other groups converged.

Mangos led them further west, from *holmen* to *holmen,* the pursuit getting closer and more numerous.

"Not that way!" Kat shouted.

Mangos stopped at the beginning of a long bridge. There was no other way off the opposite *holmen.*

An arrow buzzed past, glancing off the rock at his feet. A bowman stood on the only other bridge, drawing another arrow.

There were three ways off the *holmen*: one blocked by a bowman, one led to a dead end, and a mob of angry men closed from the way they had come.

Mangos rushed the bowman, shouting wildly. The man shrank away, his eyes wide, as he loosed his arrow.

"Give way." Mangos swung his spear like a stave, knocking the man aside and jarring the bow from his hands. He rushed past, only pausing to ensure Kat followed. The way to the western bridge was clear.

The long bridge bounced under their feet. The arm of the valley neared.

Mangos's foot shot through a board, he lurched, hitting the bridge hard, knocking the air from his lungs and wrenching his leg. He pulled himself forward, jerking his leg out of the hole. "By the gods of Eastwarn!" he swore. He tried to bend his leg, but pain shot through his thigh. He reached up to grab the hand rope. Kat grabbed him under his shoulder and yanked him up.

"Run!" she urged him.

Using his spear as a crutch, Mangos ran as well as he could. The pursuing men slowed to cross the gap he had made, so Kat and he reached the end of the bridge well ahead of them.

The only path along the valley arm was a narrow, rocky trail; the fall off into the valley was harrowing, the slope to the top of the valley's arm unclimbable.

A half-dozen men crossed the eastern bridge and turned toward them, blocking the path.

"Left!" Kat called. "Go left!"

There didn't seem to be much choice. Mangos turned toward Talhorn Mountain.

The trail narrowed as they approached the face of Talhorn. The sound of the wind ripping through the Devil's Arse grew louder.

Muscles aching, breath laboring, Mangos followed Kat up the trail. Shouts and footsteps grew closer, and he didn't want to look back. He wished he knew where the trail led, besides up.

The air felt cooler as the wind eddied around the ice ledge. They were beside it now, a dirty white projection, impossibly large, like a giant growth.

They reached the ledge proper. It wasn't a solid sheet, as Mangos had supposed, but was riddled with cracks and fissures from the summer heat. "You're not thinking of crossing this."

"You want to stop and die?" Kat tested the ice.

37

A thin layer of meltwater made the surface slick. Mangos's feet slid, and he found himself leaning on the spear, going too slowly, he thought, and a glance back confirmed that their pursuers were only a dozen yards behind.

Mangos could almost feel the ice shake from the force of the wind passing beneath it. The ledge sloped down, just a little, and it didn't take much imagination to envision sliding off into space to ride the wind until dropping seven thousand feet. The sharp edge looked too much like a knife.

Somebody screamed. Mangos snapped his head sideways and watched one of their pursuers slide down the ledge, scrambling to catch hold. The man gathered speed as he neared the edge and launched into the air where he and his screams were lost in the howling wind.

Mangos swallowed hard.

They neared the highest point on the ledge, and he realized the tremors were not his imagination. The fissures here ran deep. While the far side was only sixty yards away, he could not see a trail.

"Give me your keg," Kat shouted over the wind.

"What?"

"Give me the keg!"

Mangos shrugged off his pack and opened it. "How did you know I had one?"

"How could I not? It weighs your pack like a lead bar and gurgles when you run."

She took the keg of alcohol, fumbling a little from its weight, to a fissure near the mountain's face.

The men were nearer, jeering and threatening, but walking carefully on the slick ice. They did not need to hurry.

Kat lifted the keg and smashed it in the fissure.

"Hey!" shouted Mangos, but she ignored him. She tore the end from her shirt and took a fire starter from her pack. She squeezed the handles, making sparks fly. After several tries, she caught the rag on fire and tossed it into the fissure. She jumped back as flames and heat roared out after her.

"You're burning—"

"Time to go," Kat said. "If this works, we don't want to be here."

Mangos took the hint. He reversed his spear, took two steps and drove it into the ice, pushing himself forward. He threw himself down, sliding by their pursuers who, taken by surprise, could only flail wildly and curse as he shot past.

He pulled himself off the ice the same time as Kat. He didn't need to be told to run.

A crack, like the crack of an angry god's whip, ripped through the air. Mangos turned in time to see the ice ledge slide down the face of the mountain. There was a grumbling, a rumbling, as it twisted and began to crumble.

The men grabbed whatever they could, but it all fell with them. If they screamed, the fall of the ice covered it.

"By the gods of Eastwarn," Mangos whispered, though that, too, was drowned out.

When the last rocks and chunks of ice settled, it was silent.

Silent.

No shouts. No screams. No wind.

Mangos looked down at the mass now plugging the Devil's Arse. "There are a dozen men in there." He looked at Kat, shocked that they could have been so quickly wiped away.

It seemed the ice fall had sucked all the sound from the valley and it was only slowly coming back. The remaining men on the *holmen* murmured to each other, casting black looks at Mangos and Kat, but nothing more.

"You killed my men," Harlin said, his face full of fury.

"We're here to get paid," Kat said.

Mangos spun to look at her in surprise. "What?"

"Paid? For killing my men?" Harlin growled like an angry dog.

"For solving your problem," Kat said. "You said you didn't care how we did it."

"I didn't expect you to kill *my* men."

"You shouldn't be surprised," Kat retorted. "Bring our pay. I'll explain."

Mangos couldn't figure what might have changed other than a dozen men dying in an avalanche. That hadn't affected Lijas at all.

Harlin grumbled as he followed them over the bridges until they reached Lijas' *holmen*.

"You're here to kill me," Lijas said, holding up his crossbow. "You're right, though, the one I'd choose to kill is Harlin."

"What? You treacherous scum!" Harlin ducked behind Mangos.

"I didn't bring him for you to kill," Kat said. "You are to agree not to gather ridge berries from the ridge or any *holmen*."

"In return for my life?" Lijas curled his lip.

Kat turned, shielding her hands from Harlin, and pointed down. Lijas furrowed his brow. Kat pointed down again, then toward Talhorn. Lijas half-turned to look at the mountain.

With a sudden smile, Lijas cleared his throat. "Ah, yes, I'll not gather any berries from the ridge, or the *holmen*."

Mangos blinked. He opened his mouth in surprise and snapped it shut. He wanted to ask why, but didn't trust himself to speak.

"You mean that?" Harlin stepped out from behind Mangos. "Of course. You're not stupid. Good." He scratched his head. "Very good." He glared at Lijas. "Don't think of changing your mind."

Lijas lifted a hand and shook his head. "It's all yours."

Harlin sniffed. "Make sure you remember it." A sly smile crossed his face as he regarded Kat and Mangos. "I can get new men. Well done." He reached into his tunic and drew out a small flask. "Here you are—a royal reward."

Mangos took it. "What is this?"

But Harlin had already turned away and crossed to the next *holmen*.

"What is this?" Mangos repeated.

"A royal reward," Lijas said. "A quart of Royal Dye."

"*Dye?* We risked our lives for a quart of dye?" He drew back his hand to fling it off the *holmen*, but Kat gently took it from him.

"We may as well keep it," she said. "It is rare, after all."

Mangos rolled his eyes and turned to Lijas. The vintner stood with his crossbow pointed down, staring after Harlin.

Lijas laughed, softly. There was no chance Harlin could hear. "Ah, Harlin, you poor fool!" He laughed again, dropping his crossbow. "Come!" He beckoned to Mangos and Kat. He clapped each on the back as they stepped from the bridge. "You two may as well have worked for me!"

"What will you do now?" Mangos asked.

"Do? I have the whole valley!" Lijas threw out his arms and smiled broadly. "Think of it! Hundreds of years of guano building up! And now that there is no wind, I can plant Ridge Berry bushes. I will have the entire valley, while Harlin is stuck on these tiny little *holmen*!"

Incredulous, Mangos started to laugh as well. The sun was setting, silhouetting the solid bulk of Talhorn, the mysterious hole plugged by the avalanche.

"It will take a few years before the bushes are old enough to produce berries, and I'll want to hire guards in case Harlin dislikes our arrangement," Lijas said. He shrugged. "But come, my friends. Harlin has given you a royal reward, let me give you an Imperial one."

Mangos grinned. "I'll drink to that."

# The Sword of the Mongoose

*Six months after the fall of Alness.*

Mangos moved his Mage forward. "The black Monarch has been defeated." He leaned back and grinned. "That's everybody, gentlemen. Pay up." He enjoyed the disgruntled muttering and the chink of silver from the losers.

He swept four small piles of coins into his pouch. It was good to win. Regum had *style*, sophistication. He winked at his partner, Kat, sure she would be impressed, before turning to the fifth player.

"I, ah," the merchant licked his lips, his eyes darted around the common room, obviously aware of everybody's interest, before settling back on Mangos, "don't have the money."

An appreciative murmur seemed to curl through the room like smoke from the fire. Men looked up from their ales, some nudged neighbors who hadn't heard. Regum was an entertaining game, but it became better when it led to a blood feud. The immediate consensus was that Mangos could crush the welshing merchant, but opinion was divided on whether he could get the value of the bet.

"You must have been sure you'd win," Kat purred as she circled the table, drawing the merchant's gaze until his head turned so far he had to snap it back the other way like an owl. But in this case he looked more like a mouse than an owl.

"My debt's not to you," the merchant said. "*You* didn't even play."

"*I* did," Mangos said, nodding to the Regum board. "And I won." It surprised him this scrawny little man would risk cheating. "Do you have silver teeth? I can take those." By custom, he was within his rights to kill the man.

The merchant licked his lips. "Better. I didn't want to do this, but I'll pay you with a story. A story and a Marin sword."

Mangos narrowed his eyes. "Stories don't buy ale." But a Marin sword... that was something else altogether.

"Listen and decide." The merchant's eyes flickered around. Kat stood between him and the door. "Let me tell you of a man in

trouble," he began, and the crowd leaned forward to hear his words.

"And so," he concluded a few minutes later, "the Earl of Riverside decided to hide his sword so the Priests of An Lorum couldn't demand it as his penance."

"As tales go, that's not a very good one," Mangos said.

"Just before crossing into An Lorum, he found a rock overlooking the river—"

"Stop!" Mangos said, slapping his palm on the table, making the coins and Regum pieces jump. He glared around the common room. All the other men hastily looked away, but Mangos wasn't fooled. "The story I will share, the sword I will not. Its location is for me alone!"

The merchant nodded. "Very well." He leaned forward and began to whisper in Mangos's ear, all about markers, locations, and keys.

"Why should we believe you?" Kat said bluntly.

"Here," the merchant passed Mangos a small bronze coin. "A *noblis* of Riverside. Not worth five silvers, but a token of my veracity." He glanced at the Regum board and sighed. "I had thought it would bring me luck."

Kat snorted. "It proves nothing."

The merchant spread his hands, palms up. He raised his voice, "Is there a soothsayer here?"

A young man cleared his throat. "I have a touch of the sight." His friends pushed him forward, no doubt hoping to know the truth as well.

The merchant spoke slowly and clearly. "After making myself familiar with the details in the story, I believe there to be a sword hidden where I described, and that it surely is a Marin blade."

Mangos looked at the soothsayer. "He is telling the truth," the young man said.

"You believe him?" Kat demanded as the tavern door slammed behind the merchant. She curled her lip, making her opinion clear.

"It's not impossible, and you heard the soothsayer," Mangos said. He idly played with the bronze *noblis* as he thought of the merchant's story. The Earl of Riverside had died in the Priests' dungeon where he scratched his secret on the wall.

"It's not likely," Kat said, still standing. "He writes in code, and a hundred years later *this* merchant buys the information from another prisoner who broke the code?"

"Still," Mangos said, "a Marin sword. Do you have any idea what one is worth?"

"More than a five-silver tavern bet," Kat retorted.

"I could have killed him," Mangos said, tapping a coin on the tabletop. "It's worth his life."

"You still can kill him. If you want to go after the sword, you should catch him to keep as guide and hostage."

"Either the sword is there or it isn't," Mangos said. "Unless I want to kill him if it isn't, it makes no sense to take him hostage." He saw Kat's expression and laughed. "Isn't the lure of adventure worth five silvers? Besides, I have no wish to be knifed as I sleep.

"Marin made the first silvecite-alloyed swords," Mangos continued. How could he explain what that meant to a collector? He prided himself on knowing his steel. "Not only are Marin swords strong, well edged, and perfectly balanced, they're works of art."

"Which means you won't find them hidden alongside the road."

Mangos shook his head slowly. Owning a Marin sword would mark him as a dangerous man, a man of success and refinement. It was everything he wanted when they went to Alomar, for it would smooth his way in the city. "It doesn't hurt to check," he mused.

Kat snorted and flipped her hair back as if to say, *It's your call.* "The soothsayer did verify his words." She contemplated the Regum board. "He must have really believed he could win."

Mangos laughed. "But he didn't, and now I have his secret."

Kat lowered her voice. "The others heard the tale, and that the sword lies under a rock just this side of An Lorum. That's a very small area to look."

Mangos stood up. Only he knew the markers, but Kat was right, it was a small enough area that others would try their luck. "Let's hurry," he said.

66I'd expect a dozen men, plus whatever friends and cousins they can enlist," Mangos said. He could see two ahead of them, local youths of the sort who might go off adventuring to avoid farm work. They started to run when they saw Mangos and Kat. He wasn't worried. The boys couldn't run for three days.

He knew of others behind, men who hung back but would pass them at first opportunity. Pass them, or, when the stakes were as high as a Marin sword, kill them.

"Shall we step up the pace?" Kat asked, her tone light.

To answer, Mangos lengthened his stride. They started to gain on the boys who, when they noticed, began to run again. It became almost a game. The boys would run until they tired, then Mangos and Kat would close the gap, and the boys would run again. Each run was shorter, each time the gap closed more until Mangos and Kat passed them. The boys, red-faced and panting, shook their heads and turned for home.

"The others won't give up so easily," Kat said.

They might not, Mangos thought, but he was confident once he had a Marin sword he could best any living man.

The land rolled ahead of them, green grass cropped short by sheep and spotted with grey boulders. There were few trees and they could see for miles.

The sun outstripped them and retired for the night, but they kept moving by moonlight. Only when the moon set did they take shelter behind a large rock.

Early morning light woke Mangos. Some silent sense made him nervous, and he nudged Kat awake with his foot. Her eyes flew open, and she sat up and looked around.

A hawk cried.

"Just a hawk," Mangos said, feeling relieved.

"A white merlin? That's a noble bird. It doesn't belong to some local youth. Somebody else has gotten word of your Marin sword. I'd guess they're late to the chase, but probably mounted."

"That's *my* sword," Mangos said with righteous indignation. "I won the Regum game."

Kat didn't answer. Mangos dug in his pack for food as they started walking again.

The white merlin disappeared, but hours later it was back, circling. Kat stopped, breathing heavily, and looked back. "Look behind us."

A man and his dog stalked them several miles back, a couple miles behind him a group of four men walked, and another three beyond them. But far, far back, just visible at the top of the furthest ridge, rode a dozen horsemen.

The group of three had disappeared, and the four fallen further back. The man and his dog were now two valleys back, but the horsemen were only three ridges back, and Mangos was tired. He leaned over, hands on his knees as he tried to catch his breath.

"We're going to have to rest," he said. Kat nodded, too winded to speak.

Clouds were gathering and he wondered where they came from. He had not noticed them blowing in. In spite of his words, he started down into the next valley, pushed by the images of the horsemen.

Another road ran along the valley floor and intersected their road. A wagon sat at the crossroads. The horse, a dun mare, drank at a stone trough while a man rubbed it down. Battered pots and worn tools hung from the wagon's sides. Mangos could see other goods, all used, inside the canvas cover.

When the man saw them he dropped his rag and drew a curved sword. He called to somebody out of sight and a woman's voice answered.

"She's Alnessi," murmured Kat as she glanced up at the clouds and raised her hood.

Refugees. The fall of Alness had scattered her citizens across the world. That was why they were selling junk. Likely they scavenged their goods as they fled their country.

"Merchants," Mangos said as a man moved between them and the wagon.

"Barely merchants," Kat said, "and they're worried about us being bandits."

"We've nothing you want," called out the man, his voice accented.

*That's pretty clear*, Mangos thought. "We weren't planning on taking any of it." *How do they sell anything if they don't have anything people want?*

Kat turned so she faced Mangos but had her back to the others. "He's Hafizi," she murmured, but Mangos didn't know who the Hafizi were or why one would be travelling with an Alnessi merchant. "Dangerous."

"Wait," Mangos said. "Maybe we do want something. Which way are you going?"

"South," said a woman, stepping out from behind the wagon. She was barely a woman, a girl really, and looked thin and worn.

"We'll pay you to take us west," Mangos said.

"No," the man said.

"Celzez," the woman said with a wave for him to keep quiet. "How far, and how much?"

"Twenty, twenty-five miles," Mangos said. "We'll pay five silvers."

There was a certain symmetry in five silvers, the value of the tale.

"Take us two days out of our way for five silvers?" The girl snorted.

"One day," Mangos protested.

"Two, we have to come back."

Overhead, the merlin cried.

"Ten silvers," Mangos shrugged.

"Twenty."

A few heavy drop of rain fell, raising puffs of dust on the road. Mangos glanced behind them. "But we travel quickly, no lagging."

The girl nodded. "I'm Jalani. This is Celzez. Climb on."

Mangos settled in the back, trying to find space among the junk. The wagon might travel slowly, but at least they could rest as it moved.

"You're Alnessi?" Mangos asked, more to fill the silence than anything else.

"I am," Jalani said. "Celzez was my father's Hafizi guard. My father was a merchant." She said the last with a note of defiance.

"You're a long way from Alness."

"Celzez saved me from the fighting, and we escaped the city," Jalani said. "We found this wagon. I suppose we stole it, though the owners were dead. The best we could do was bury them."

She snapped the reins.

"We caught the horse running wild, no idea who owned it, gathered such goods as hadn't been broken or burned and headed south. We've been living as tinkers and petty merchants ever since."

Looking around the sorry merchandise, Jalani shook her head. "A poor start to rebuilding my father's business."

Nodding absently, Mangos stared out the back. He laughed to see the first men start to run when they saw the wagon. They might gain for a bit, but the last two days travel had been brutal, they had to be as exhausted as he was. They could never keep the pace.

But further back, dust rose from the hooves of a dozen horses. They could not outrun this pursuit; they could only hope to reach the sword's hiding place first.

"That hill there," Mangos said, pointing to a low hill rising up from the valley floor below them. The rain had grown heavier the closer they came to the valley, and now it fell like a lace curtain, making everything grey and hazy.

A river meandered along the broad valley floor, passing on the far side of the hill. Dead trees dotted its banks.

A bridge, long, old, and solid, spanned the river, the top of its arch visible above the hill. Just upstream a tower perched on a rocky island; the flood line of discolored stone was higher than the first floor.

Mangos studied the bridge and tower. "No doubt at all." He turned his attention back to the hill, searching for signs of the sword's hiding place.

"They're close," Kat said, pointing to the horsemen behind.

"Faster!" Mangos urged Jalani.

"No faster," Jalani answered. "Speed downhill will ruin a horse."

Mangos jumped from the wagon. "We can go faster on foot." He began to run.

"Hey!" shouted Jalani. "You still have to pay us!"

"Meet us on that small hill!" Mangos shouted back. He slipped in the mud but kept running.

At the top of the hill, Kat looked around. "You said there should be a marker stone..." She trailed away as she searched the tall grass and short bushes along the side of the road.

The tower stood closer now, three levels of dark stone with slate shutters and roof. The shutters of the first level were closed, but an unnatural glow came from the open windows of the top floor.

The rain had found the seam between Mangos's hood and his cape. He could feel the wetness seeping down his back. Mangos shuddered, not sure if it were the blue glow or the cold rain that sent shivers down his spine. He reminded himself that a Marin sword equaled respect. By owning one he would command better jobs and higher pay. The drinks and pleasurable company would come easy. *Alomar will swoon at my feet,* he thought.

"Over here," Kat called.

Mangos hurried over. Wet grass obscured the overturned road marker. "Now to find the first stone. Ten paces east," he said, starting to walk the distance, "two paces south." He stopped beside a large stone. "Roll the stone." He dried his hands on the front of his tunic where it was still dry and took a grip on the stone. With a heave, he rolled it over.

There was a small cavity underneath with a largish piece of stone inside. At first glance it looked like whatever was hidden there had been taken and the side collapsed, but Mangos knew he needed the stone. He picked it up and grinned at Kat. "Just like we were told."

Kat nodded. "Hurry."

The horsemen were halfway down the valley—close enough to see the riders' armor and weapons.

Mangos carried the stone to the other side of the road, closer to where the tower brooded over the river, the blue light even more ominous in the heavy rain.

"It should be over here somewhere," he said, looking over the stones on the top of the hill. He paced around one, examining it from every side.

"It can't be this easy," Kat said.

Mangos pushed the stone. It wouldn't move. He moved to another spot and took a better grip. He couldn't budge the stone. "I *should* be able to move that," he said. He brushed some water from a small depression, an action that had no discernable effect.

He set the stone from under the first rock on the second stone, wiggling it until it settled snugly into the depression. He couldn't repress a grin.

The stone rolled easily with his next effort. He held his breath as a cavity came into view.

There *was* a sword.

And it was beautiful. The blade was straight and true, without the least sign of rust. The guard was skillfully fashioned to look spare and elegant but still protect his hand. The pommel looked to be a work of art. He reached down to pick up the sword and examined it more closely.

"It looks like a Marin sword," he breathed as he lifted the sword from the ground.

A thunderous crack exploded overhead, and the sky opened up. Rain fell in torrents, so hard it weighed on his head and shoulders. He couldn't see the bridge, the tower, or the wagon. He could barely see Kat standing beside him.

Nonetheless he swung the sword, cutting through the rain and marveling at its balance. He squinted at the pommel and ran his hand along the flat of the blade.

"It's real!" he exulted. "A true Marin blade!"

Wealth, respect, power—Mangos held it all in his hand. Even in corrupt Alomar, a Marin sword would turn heads.

"Too easy," Kat muttered. She paced away but returned to look at the sword. "Still too easy." She shook her head.

Mangos laughed and swung the sword again.

The rain slackened.

Kat froze. "You'll want to look at this."

Mangos lowered the sword and followed her gaze. The river had jumped its banks and was flooding around the approach to the bridge. It rose as he watched, climbing further. The rain dripping down his back felt unusually cold. "That's not natural," he said.

The water already rushed over the roadway. The dead trees stuck from the water like claws with white ribbon cuffs of whitewater trailing downstream.

Mangos shuddered at the mere thought of swimming that flood. "We can't go that way."

"Or back."

Mangos turned. The flood had flanked the hill and was rioting across the valley, turning the boulder-strewn ground into a treacherous mass of swirling white water.

Caught at the far edge of the flood, the horsemen scrambled back up the valley side. On the near side, Jalani and Celzez coaxed and prodded their tired horse to climb faster.

As one, Mangos and Kat turned to look at the tower. The blue light pierced the still heavy rain.

"I'd like to be a little further away from that," Mangos said.

"Cut the horse free!" Kat yelled to Jalani. The flood already lapped at the wagon's back wheels.

Jalani shook her head, but Celzez drew his curved sword and cut the traces. The wagon rolled back and freed the horse from the shafts. The flood lifted the back end of the wagon and pulled it completely into the water. It turned as it moved downstream, briefly hanging up on a tree before breaking free and rushing away.

"So," said Celzez. "We are here. Are we to just wait to drown?"

Mangos turned completely around. It seemed likely. The water raged over the abutments of the bridge, it swirled above the door on the tower, and it climbed the slopes of the hill where he stood.

"What's that?" He pointed to the tower where something moved.

The door opened, a glowing portal under the flood.

"Magic," hissed Jalani.

The water before them swirled. A hole opened in the center, and the water spun outward, revealing a tunnel stretching out toward the tower.

Far down the tunnel, shadows moved, shuffling forward to resolve into the forms of men.

The men's faces were pale and waxy, blemished by scrapes, bites, and gouges. Black and bloated hands hung like blood sausages from the ends of their arms.

Kat hissed, a sound of surprise and revulsion. "Revenants!"

Undead servants of a necromancer. Mangos felt a chill in his guts.

A dozen revenants issued from the tunnel and circled the hill. Their complete indifference to the rain, the mud, and anything the living could do, was harrowing. The final revenant, a man who must have been a smith in life, judging from his leather trousers and apron, lifted a black hand and pointed to the tunnel.

The merchant gulped. "Maybe the necromancer is offering us sanctuary."

"That's a sanctuary I don't want to take," Kat said.

"We may not have a choice," Mangos replied.

Jalani jerked her head up and down, sending drops of water flying. "I think we should risk it. The upper levels of that tower should be safe."

"Not safe," Mangos and Kat said at the same time.

The revenants took a step forward, and the dead smith pointed again.

"Celzez?" Jalani asked.

"We should not go down that tunnel," Celzez said. He swung his sword through the rain. "We should kill them here."

"They're already dead," Jalani said. Her voice cracked as the revenants took another step closer.

Mangos stabbed the one nearest him. His Marin sword slid in easily, a blow that would have killed a man. The revenant pawed at the sword like it wanted to push it away.

"Don't make them angry!" the merchant moaned.

The revenants took another step, and the smell of rot and mold washed over them. With a whimper, Jalani broke away and slipped and slithered through the mud to the tunnel.

"Jalani!" called Celzez. "Jalani!" He hurried after her.

"Damn," muttered Kat.

"It's Hell and high water here," Mangos said. He jerked his sword free. "Maybe the Necromancer does offer safety," he said, though he didn't believe it.

"No. He doesn't. They never do." Kat twisted away from a revenant as it stepped forward, but there was another beside it. They stood shoulder to shoulder, two deep in places, and behind them the water still rose.

"Let's go," Mangos said. "Even if we could kill them, we can't escape the flood."

It was like stepping inside a waterspout laid on its side. Water twisted around them, it sounded angry. Only an inch of sorcery held back death, and Mangos had little faith in it.

They went single file, for only a narrow strip of ground showed at the bottom, and nobody seemed inclined to step on the curved water walls that somehow circled the tunnel in spite of intersecting the ground. The revenants clustered behind them, expressionless, crowding them forward.

"Necromancers," Mangos muttered, aware of the stink, but not knowing if it came from the revenants or the river muck. "He's not making a good impression."

"They never do," Kat said. "They live on the borders, just close enough to grab people to use in their magic but far enough away to avoid important people's wrath."

Jalani and Celzez hesitated to climb out of the riverbed to the glowing door, but the revenants kept coming, dragging their feet through the mud and puddles. Even worse, the far end of the tunnel had collapsed and brown, frothing water followed the revenants toward them. "We can't stay here," Mangos said.

Celzez lifted Jalani up the riverbank. Kat followed. Mangos gave the revenants and the shortening tunnel one last look before climbing up and entering the necromancer's tower.

The door slammed shut, and water boomed against it as the tunnel completely collapsed. Water trickled around the frame, darkening the wood.

Silence, then the plink of water dripped from the rocks. The room was empty except for a set of stairs coiling up the far side of the tower to the next floor.

The revenants leaned against the outer wall and slumped, all semblance of life leaving them. Now they were just corpses piled against the walls, flaccid and motionless, all staring eyes, slack jaws, and rivulets of dried blood.

"We're underwater," Jalani said, looking very young and very scared.

*We were before*, Mangos thought, but didn't say it.

The water plinked again.

Black iron lanterns held globes of blue light. It gave the others a pale, sickly hue. *No different than the revenants. Is this what we'll become?* he wondered.

"I, ah, don't much like it here," Jalani said.

"We'll like it less when it floods," Celzez said. He stomped his foot and water splashed.

"We'd best be moving up," Kat said. She put action to her words, going over to the stairs.

Mangos gestured Jalani and Celzez forward. He followed them up, only stopping once to watch the water creeping over the corpses.

Kat was already prowling the second floor.

Shelves of bottles and boxes lined the tower. More bottles covered a table in the center of the room, and strings of dried...stuff—Mangos didn't know what it might be—hung from the ceiling. It still smelled of decay, but of spice and ash and something animal as well.

"Dragon's blood," Kat said as she studied the rows of bottles. "Tanis leaf. Heela spikes—that's impressive."

"You know these things?" Jalani asked.

Kat nodded. "Very rare, very dangerous, very expensive."

Jalani nodded, exhaustion etched on her face. She sank into a black chair half hidden by the table.

"Don't sit there!"

Jalani jumped up. Kat shook her head. "Arcane." She drew their attention to a large basin behind the chair with her sword point. "Quicksilver." She then pointed to a giant stone font. A wooden lid covered it. As she took the lid, she closed her eyes as if overcome with emotion. "Life," she said, "This is where the necromancer harvests his victims' lives to fuel his magic."

A warm yellow glow filled the room.

The lid slammed closed, seemingly by itself. Kat tried to open it again, but her hand slipped off.

"Do not touch what does not belong to you." A cloaked and hooded figure stood on the stairs to the third level.

"Then you shouldn't leave it out," Kat said. "It isn't really yours. It belongs to those downstairs."

"You criticize me? Do you not know who I am?" He lifted both hands to lower his hood. It was the story-telling merchant from the inn.

Mangos felt his jaw drop open and he closed it with a snap. "Damn you! This was all to trap us?"

"Not just you," the necromancer said. "That story was aimed at every adventurer in the room. But," he shrugged, "you carried the trigger for the flood."

Mangos thought of the bronze *noblis* he carried. Then another thought crossed his mind. "You owe me five silver pieces!"

"Fool!" roared the necromancer. "I am the right hand of Death himself."

Jalani let out a soft whimper. Celzez stood in front of her. His hand shook as he lifted his sword.

"I am the devourer of souls!" roared the necromancer.

It seemed the darkness in the nooks of the tower grew deeper.

"I am the render of the creation." The man's words shook the very air.

"You own the tower where I'll be staying until the waters recede," Mangos said.

"I am ISAK YAN!" the necromancer shouted. "The waters recede when I say they'll recede, and you'll be staying much longer than that."

"Will you be serving dinner?"

"I don't think," said the necromancer, "you appreciate what is about to become of your life."

*I think I do*, thought Mangos, feeling the ice in his stomach and what felt like spiders walking on the back of his neck. *But if he can try to scare us, I can laugh at him.* Yet while Mangos felt scared, the necromancer wasn't laughing.

Isak Yan pointed to Jalani. "You are about to replenish my cauldron. Sit." When Jalani didn't move he said, "All I need do is call the revenants."

Keeping one eye on Isak Yan, Mangos went to the stairs. Something moved in the blue water, shadows that resolved into men and began to climb toward the surface.

The first revenant rose up, water dripping. Mangos slashed, opening a large gash that did nothing to slow it. He kicked it back into the water, but two more replaced it. He had to retreat.

The revenants were stiff and awkward but deceptively fast. While two attacked Mangos, others rushed past.

Celzez defended Jalani while Kat carved the hands from a revenant threatening her.

Isak Yan stood above them, watching. He lifted a hand.

Mangos's vision swirled, and the world tilted. The ground wasn't where his feet were, or so it seemed, and he fell. Across the room he saw Celzez fall before revenant feet, black and scabby, blocked his vision.

He rolled and rose, lurching and flailing as the room swam. "Beware sorcery!" he shouted as swung, somehow separating a revenant's head from its neck.

Kat dropped her sword and grabbed two large flasks from the table.

"No!" shouted Isak Yan. Mangos's balance returned as Isak Yan faced Kat and lifted his arms above his head. His hands sparkled as he thrust them toward Kat. Kat smashed one flask before the sparks enveloped her like a swarm of fireflies. The little, twinkling lights settled on her and she slowed and stopped moving, the second flask tilted and her free hand reaching for her dagger.

Isak Yan lifted his sleeve to mop his face.

A sharp scream pierced the air. Jalani struggled in the grip of a revenant while Celzez tried futilely to reach her.

"Give up," Isak Yan said.

"Not likely." Nearly surrounded, Mangos could only put the stairwell at his back and try to keep the revenants from grappling him.

Cold hands grabbed his wrists. A revenant climbing from below pulled his arms back. He felt cold, wet flesh pressing against his back, and the stench of rot filled his nostrils. He struggled, but the hands pinching his wrists, hard bone gripping through flaccid muscles, held him tight.

"You see how fruitless your struggle is?" Isak Yan said.

Mangos kicked backwards, hoping to catch the revenant holding him by surprise. He struck hard, but with no result.

"It doesn't seem you do. You'd better bring me his sword." Isak Yan gestured and a revenant tore the sword from Mangos's grip.

"Give it back!" Mangos shouted, renewing his struggle. The Marin blade was irreplaceable!

Isak Yan came down and took the blade. He turned it over and held it up to the light. "Very, very nice. You are, indeed, a man of taste and accomplishment," he mocked. He laid it on the table. "It shall go back in the ground for the next adventurer to find."

"Fool to bury it!" Mangos snarled. He needed a sword; he wanted that one.

Isak Yan shrugged. "Telling the truth helps lure otherwise suspicious folk."

Mangos lunged forward, but again could not break free. He could not expect help, either. Kat strained against the magic holding her, but couldn't do more than quiver. Four revenants hemmed in Celzez, and Jalani could not break free of the revenant holding her.

"Bring me the girl," Isak Yan commanded.

The revenant dragged Jalani over to the ebony chair.

Isak Yan came down the stairs, extended his hands over the bowl of quicksilver, and began to murmur arcane words.

Mist gathered over the bowl, silver and faintly luminous. It grew thick and began to swirl, spinning into threads and from threads into ropes.

Jalani moaned as the ropes drifted to her, wrapping around her arms and legs, binding her to the chair. She closed her eyes and seemed to grow smaller as she shrank back.

Isak Yan drew a long, black knife. He reached into a dark corner and seemed to cut the air. He pulled back a piece of darkness and pulled it over Jalani's head.

*A hood of shadows,* Mangos thought.

Celzez roared, bashing aside the revenants in front of him and rushing at Isak Yan. He raised his curved sword as he attacked.

Isak Yan lifted his other hand. "You...can't...win," he said, his teeth clenched and muscles tight.

Celzez slowed, as if he pushed against greater and greater resistance. He started to swing his sword, but it moved with glacial slowness and finally stopped altogether.

Isak Yan quivered with the effort of all his magic.

Kat's hand shook. The liquid in the flask she held crept over the lip. A thick, syrupy fluid, it caught the light as it stretched, slowly, to the floor. Smoke twisted up as it touched the spilled contents of the flask she dropped earlier.

The two liquids exploded, lifting Kat from her feet and throwing her across the room. The blast cleared everything from the table. Heat washed across Mangos.

With a cry of exertion, Mangos flexed to free himself. The revenant clung to his wrists; he was pulling it more tightly against his back. With an awful tearing sound, he pulled free.

He had torn off the revenant's arms; they still clung to his wrists.

He started to use them to club the revenants around him.

58

"Kill the necromancer," Kat said. She climbed to her feet, clothes singed and a dazed expression on her face.

*With these weapons?* Mangos wondered. *At least I'm armed.*

He knocked the revenants back, but couldn't stop them. The Marin sword had been lost in the explosions, blown somewhere out of sight. Kat had taken Celzez's sword and cut the head from a revenant, but she was barely holding back several others.

"I don't want them to kill you," Isak Yan said.

*He just wants to kill us himself.* Mangos needed to attack the necromancer directly, for the revenants would eventually win. He could not outlast the undead.

He avoided the blundering charge of an armless revenant. *Madness,* he thought. His eye settled on a sword hilt amongst the mess on the floor—his Marin blade.

Mangos dove forward and grabbed the sword; it settled into his hand, feeling like an extension of his arm. It was perfectly balanced, perfectly proportioned. *A man could do amazing things with this,* he thought.

Mangos uncoiled in a lunge, stretching as far as he could, and was rewarded by striking Isak Yan. Isak Yan parried too late, swiping after the sword had sunk deep into his chest.

The black knife cracked against the Marin blade. The knife dissolved into shadows that disappeared in the corners of the room. The Marin blade vibrated, letting off a low moan before it shattered.

Isak Yan gasped, and all motion stopped.

The revenants collapsed, the quicksilver ropes binding Jalani splashed to the floor, and the hood of shadows disappeared.

Isak Yan hunched over, clutching at his chest as if he could draw out the portion of blade still inside him. He dropped to his knees and collapsed completely.

"He broke my sword," Mangos said, staring at the hilt in disbelief.

Kat nodded. She went over to the window and opened the shutter a crack.

"He broke my sword," Mangos repeated.

"I heard you." Kat opened the shutter wide. "It stopped raining."

"That sword was worth a fortune."

Jalani blinked in the light. She seemed dazed. "You saved my life."

"But you cost her the wagon and all her trade goods," Celzez said.

"I lost my sword," Mangos said.

Kat stared at both of them and started to prowl the room. "Sell

this," she told Jalani. "Instead of that junk you had, sell all of this."
She stopped by the font. "Even the life essence."

Celzez protested, "We only want the value of what we lost. This is
worth much, much more."

A small smile stole over Kat's lips, "Are you on her side or not?
We're adventurers, not merchants; and you fought the battle too."

Their conversation barely registered with Mangos as he gathered
the shards of his Marin blade. He cupped them carefully in his hands,
thinking how few they seemed. He took them to the window and
threw them into the receding flood.

# The Valley of Terzol

*Eight months after the fall of Alness.*

"**D**o you think it's poisonous?" Mangos asked, prodding the snake with the tip of his sword.

"Almost everything else in this jungle is, why not that?" Kat answered.

Mangos laughed. The snake coiled and hissed, its white mouth contrasting sharply with its vivid green and yellow skin. It had inch-long fangs that folded up as it drew back and closed its mouth.

"It'd make a nice belt," Mangos said as he tapped the snake under the chin. The coil became a mass of frenzied movement, and there were three sharp "clacks" as it struck the sword. Mangos stepped back. The snake coiled and struck again, but Mangos twisted his sword, and the snake's head hit the ground and rolled away while the body thrashed on the jungle floor.

Kat cut away some branches at the far side of the clearing and glanced over her shoulder at him. "You may as well bring it now."

"Will you stop playing?" said a waspish voice. Andorholm Wallenoop stood up and wiped sweat from his face. "It's like I brought a child."

"If you're ready to go," said Mangos.

Andor snorted and jerked his head in a way that managed to say, 'It wasn't my idea to rest' when, in fact, it had been. Mangos and Kat had to slow considerably so they wouldn't outpace their employer.

Andor claimed to be an adventurer, but his skin was too pale, his hands too soft, and he cared about little inconveniences too much.

"I didn't bring you to play with snakes," said Andor peevishly. "I brought you to protect me." He looked at Kat. "I'm not even sure why I brought you. I don't even desire you."

Mangos sucked in his breath. In less than a year since he and Kat met, they had become known as a clever and dangerous team. He knew little of Kat's background, but he knew of her abilities. Andor was a fool to disparage her, but Kat merely looked at him, a slight flaring of her nostrils her only reaction.

"Had I known the Meerkat was a woman," Andor went on, "I would have sought my bodyguards elsewhere."

"Have a care, little man," said Mangos. "Lest we return your money and leave you here."

"Oh, I'll keep you on," Andor retorted. "I've come this far."

"And how much further?" inquired Mangos, glad to change the subject. Kat still had not spoken.

Andor snorted. "You needn't know."

"We'll know when we get there," Mangos huffed.

Andor curled his lip. "I doubt you would recognize it even then."

"We're in the Terzol Valley," said Kat, her arm raised to cut another branch. Mangos blinked.

Andor swiveled his head and looked at her for a long moment before speaking. "We are."

"As Terzol is the heart of the world, so the Emperor's house is the heart of Terzol," she continued. It sounded like a quote. "He controlled religion, government, and commerce. We're going to the Imperial Palace."

Andor licked his lips. "That need not concern you," he said.

"Terzol is—" started Mangos.

"Not a myth," interjected Kat. She swung her machete and a branch fell to the ground. "Your people never had much commerce with them."

"I never said it was a myth," said Mangos, offended. He came from Arnelan, a narrow strip of land between the Western Sea and Callos Mountains. With fish, farm, and mines at hand, they needed little. Mangos only knew Terzol as an Empire months to the east that had fallen centuries before.

It wasn't that he had anything against learning. He even planned to get some sometime. And, if he was completely honest, he was a little jealous of Kat's knowledge. "I just wondered who said Terzol was the heart of the world."

Kat did not answer. Mangos looked at Andor, but he didn't answer either. He was used to Kat's mysterious background. When they first met she looked so haggard he thought her an escaped slave. Later when he discovered she could fight, he revised his opinion to escaped gladiatrix. Still later, as she haggled over supplies, he thought perhaps a merchant's guard. Now that he had seen her learning on several subjects, he admitted he didn't know what to think.

Kat beckoned with her machete, inviting Andor to precede her into the jungle.

"No," said Andor. "You go first." He glanced back the way they had come, a nervous habit that made Mangos wonder if he expected pursuit.

Kat stepped from the clearing back into the jungle.

Mangos watched her for a second before following. None could deny she was extremely beautiful. Yet he did not desire her, and it puzzled him. Since he didn't doubt his manhood, he suspected magic.

"What are you doing?" Mangos hissed. Kat was crouched over the sleeping Andor, both barely shadows under the protection of a leaning tree, several paces from the fire.

Kat didn't answer, and Mangos did not repeat his question. The long day's travel, a meal of roast snake, and a safe shelter had put Andor to sleep. His snores joined the symphony of insects to form the background noise of the jungle night. Mangos did not want to wake him.

Kat slipped back to the fire, not at all concerned.

Mangos frowned. She held a small brass scroll tube with shards of wax still clinging to grooves at one end. She worried out the wooden stopper to retrieve the scroll inside. Carefully unrolling the yellowed and flaked parchment, she turned it so it would better catch the light.

"You're reading his papers!" Mangos said.

"I got bored," said Kat with a little shrug. "Besides, he stole this from someone else."

"What if he wakes up?" But Mangos couldn't contain his curiosity. "What is it?"

"An old receipt and instructions for delivery. Very old, very fragile. My guess is the merchandise was never picked up, and Andor wants it."

"In Terzol?" Mangos flinched at the volume of his voice. He spoke more softly. "Is he mad?"

"A little, maybe," Kat replied. "But it was stored in the Palace-Temple, well protected, and could only be removed with a certain key. There is an impression on the paper where it wrapped around a seal. Again a guess, but the seal is probably the key needed to unlock a vault containing the merchandise. If the vault was hidden or strong enough, it might not have been looted."

"He has the seal?"

"I put it back around his neck this morning," Kat said; Mangos couldn't help looking at her in amazement. "What? I just wanted to look at it. It's very nice work; an antiques dealer would pay good silver for it."

Mangos thought a moment, glanced at Andor to ensure he still slept. "So what is this merchandise?"

"It doesn't say."

Mangos sat back, disappointed.

"But consider," Kat continued, "it was so valuable they would not name it in writing, and the Terzoli would not take responsibility to ship it. It is so valuable that somebody paid in full without delivery. No," she added before he could ask. "It doesn't say who paid, or how much." She rerolled the parchment and slid it back into its brass tube.

"Fools doing business," muttered Mangos.

"Fools because the Terzoli civil war made it too dangerous to fetch their merchandise." Kat smiled a smile that made her look a little feral. "Maybe somebody believed it was lost, maybe somebody died, but it was forgotten until our friend here found the receipt and key. And that," she said in a tone that suggested this was the important part, "answers why an accountant hired bodyguards to travel to Terzol."

"An accountant? How do you know he was an accountant?"

Kat laid a finger on her lips to indicate he should be quiet. She returned to Andor's side. Something in the night howled, and Andor stirred, his snoring interrupted. Kat froze. After a second, she slid the tube back into his pack and returned to the fire.

"He has ink stains on his fingers. He could be an archivist," she said as she sat down again, "but he doesn't seem the sort."

66"If you would stop looking behind us and look ahead, you might see we have a problem," Mangos said to Andor.

A group of men, all carrying sticks, formed a half circle, blocking their way. They guarded a squalid village of branch and leaf huts, arranged around a muddy clearing. Only one building was of stone, a small structure against a hill with roots crawling over and in it. Grey stone people peered between the roots, part of elaborate carvings on the walls.

"We're going that way," said Andor, pointing through the village.

The center man, apparently the leader, spoke angrily and waved his stick. Mud-covered children watched the confrontation. The small children clung to their mother's legs while the older ones stared wide-eyed and open-mouthed at Mangos and Kat.

"Do you realize," said Andor, "I don't understand a word they're saying?"

"They're talking too fast," replied Kat. "You see the leader's helmet? That's old—imperial Terzol, I'd guess. The stone building too."

The center man, the largest of what Mangos now counted was a dozen men, wore a conical bronze helmet large enough to rest on his shoulders. He peered out the arched opening in front like a bird peering from a birdhouse. He had a spearhead tied to his club and wore strips of something cut to resemble greaves, pauldrons, and bracers.

He shouted angrily and gestured to the jungle behind them.

Mangos shook his head. "We're not going back."

Just then, a little boy, maybe six years old, ran out from behind his mother and kicked Mangos. Mangos caught the boy by the hair and lifted him off the ground. He started to scream and kick, but Mangos held him at arm's length. The villagers cried out.

"Yours?" Mangos asked, raised the boy a little.

The boy's mother wailed, raising her arms in supplication and falling to her knees. One of the men took a step forward and shook his club, shouting unknown threats. Mangos shook the boy a little and said, "Now we have something to talk about."

The boy started to cry and the man with the club waved it again.

"I think," said Kat, "you have his son."

"You'll get us all killed!" cried Andor.

Mangos drew his sword and bared his teeth. "If everybody on one side dies, it won't be us."

Andor spoke, haltingly, stumbling over unfamiliar words. The villagers clearly struggled to understand him.

"What are you saying?" Mangos demanded.

Andor didn't answer but kept talking to the villagers.

"He is begging them not to kill us," said Kat. "At least I think that's what he thinks he's saying. I wouldn't use the same phrasing, but I can only read Terzoli, I can't speak it."

"We don't need to speak Terzoli!" shouted Mangos. He dropped the boy, who scrambled into his mother's arms. "Is there a man here who dares face me?"

"Don't antagonize them!" squawked Andor.

"Careful," Kat said.

One of the men lifted a short, straight stick to his mouth and blew. There was a little buzz, a flash of steel, and a clank as Kat knocked a dart from the air with her sword. Two more men lifted their blowguns.

Mangos roared and charged. The villagers scattered. Kat and Andor followed, and the three dashed into the jungle.

"Bluff and misdirection and brute force," Mangos said as they pushed through the undergrowth. He glared at Andor, "works better than begging."

The village was long behind them with no sign of pursuit when dark clouds rolled across the sky. Kat and Mangos noticed and took out their cloaks. Andor didn't notice; instead he kept looking behind them.

The rain rolled after the clouds. One moment, it was overcast; the next, rain fell in sheets. Andor hastily pulled out his own cloak.

Mangos carefully turned so Andor couldn't see his smile.

"Cursed rain!" grumbled Andor. "Why does it happen now?" He sighed, the sigh of long suffering that made Mangos want to strangle him.

"Tell me of Terzol," Mangos said as they worked their way through the sodden jungle. Conversation would distract him from the fact the rain had found the seam between his cloak and hood and now trickled down his back.

"Why?" Andor snorted. "You don't need to know to do your job."

"Terzol controlled this whole valley," said Kat. "It was all cultivated, with a half-dozen cities and an extensive canal network."

Mangos wiped the sweat from his face. "You'd never know. Those trees look hundreds of years old."

"They probably are. The empire fell three hundred fifty years ago. Civil War."

"Let me guess," Mangos said. "Armies back and forth, crops don't get planted, trade disappears. Famine, fire, and a great stillness come over the land."

"And then the jungle covers it all," Kat said. "Although you told the tale without the high drama of treachery and tragedy." He heard her laughter over the dripping water from the jungle's canopy. "Ruins litter the Terzol valley," she continued. "Ruins of an empire that tore itself apart, fighting itself back into savagery, back to primitives huddling amongst the bones of their ancestors' greatness."

"You didn't make that up," said Andor. "That is from Teritum of Alomar's *History of Terzol*."

"Hmmm," Kat noted in agreement. "Maybe you're an archivist after all."

67

Mangos and Kat stepped out from under the canopy to the edge of the canal. They faced a hundred yards of rain-splashed water. On the far side, rising over the jungle, was the top of a great building, small in the distance, but visible by its height.

"We could swim," said Kat.

"Eh." Mangos didn't like the idea but didn't want to admit it.

"You can swim, can't you?"

"Of course," replied Mangos, but he wondered if he could swim that distance and how they would get their gear across.

The sound of Andor panting interrupted further conversation. They fell silent to watch him approach the canal. The sight seemed to strike him a physical blow. His mouth opened and closed, his eyes bulged in his pale and sweaty face. He struggled to speak. "I'm not swimming that."

"Do you have a better idea?" Kat sounded angry.

Mangos shaded his eyes and looked down the canal. "We could try the bridge."

It had been a grand bridge. It once spanned the canal in three arches, two short on each side with a long center span that barges could pass beneath. Much of the marble remained, though rust bled from the joints.

A long ramp rose out of the jungle to form the abutment and lessen the incline of the road as it rose toward the top of the bridge. The first arch still stood, crossing a quarter of the canal. The center arch had fallen; it was visible under the cloudy yellow-green water. The footings for another support poked out of the water, bits of the spandrels still clinging to it, but nothing more. The last arch had also fallen, and bits of it stuck above the water, forming stepping-stones to the far side.

Upon reaching the bridge, Mangos ran his hand over the stained marble. "The re-enforcing rods are likely rusted away," he said. "They sometimes used iron cages filled with crushed rock to fill the abutments and spandrels. It was cheaper and easier than moving larger stones from the quarry."

Kat looked at him incredulously; clearly amazed he would know that, perhaps even surprised he would know the terms. "I did not know that," she said.

"My father was a mason," he said, feeling his skin redden as he blushed. "He once worked on a bridge." He changed the subject: "I think if we get to the other support, we can jump from stone to stone to the far side."

"And just how are we supposed to get there?" demanded Andor. "I told you I'm not swimming."

"If we can wedge a branch with a rope tied to it on that support, someone can pull themselves across."

"That would be me," volunteered Kat. "I'm the lightest and not afraid of water." Her smirk told Mangos she suspected why he didn't want to swim.

It took Mangos a dozen tries before he lodged a stick on the broken support. He pulled the rope tight and tied it to the abutment.

Kat pulled on the rope. "This ought to work." She slid off the edge of the bridge and started to cross, moving first one hand than the other. Her weight caused the rope to stretch and sag.

"A little lower and I may as well be swimming," she said between breaths.

As her feet dipped near the water, dozens of fish rose to the surface, making ripples as they circled below her.

"I don't think you want to do that," Mangos called. "Swim, I mean."

Kat kept moving forward, dropping even lower as she neared the midpoint. A fish leapt from the water, missed her, and splashed back. More fish started to leap, and she swayed to avoid them.

"They're—oh!" she exclaimed as a fish narrowly missed her, but bit her cape and hung, thrashing but unable to extract its teeth from the cloth. "They have large teeth."

"Hold tight, I'll raise the rope!" Mangos called. He grabbed the rope and began to pull it. At the far end the stones shifted. Kat dropped, jerked to a stop.

"Don't!" she shouted.

He stopped, unable to pull or let go while the fish kept jumping. Kat gyrated wildly as she tried to pull herself across the canal.

A huge shape, perhaps twenty feet long, swam into view just beneath the surface. It had a blunt snout, four stubby legs, and a long tail. "Not good," Mangos said, "Not at all good." The crocodile rose, its broad back breaking the surface, and swam under Kat.

The fish ignored the crocodile and kept leaping at Kat. She hung no more than a foot above the water.

The stone shifted again and Kat dropped a few more inches.

The crocodile opened its mouth, four feet long and full of teeth. It

closed it with a snap, and Kat let out a surprised cry. The crocodile turned toward the far bank then circled back.

Kat stopped struggling, lifted her feet higher, and watched it pass directly beneath her.

The stone shifted.

Kat let go.

"No!" cried Mangos. His heart seemed to stop.

Kat dropped onto the crocodile's back, ran its length and sprang into a shallow dive. She knifed into the water; the fish darted away and immediately swarmed back. The crocodile twisted around, its great tail driving it in pursuit.

Mangos could only swear, over and over, as his heart hammered. He prepared to dive in, stopped, tried again—couldn't do it.

Kat broached the water at the ruined support, pulled herself up, clothes in tatters, blood trickling through the holes. She climbed as her life depended on it, ignoring the jumping fish.

The crocodile erupted after her, teeth flashing, tail thrashing, beating the water to foam as it tried to scale the support.

And then Kat was crouched on the top, dripping water and blood, watching the crocodile scrabble uselessly. A fish flopped at her side, still caught on her cape.

Mangos let out his breath, and it seemed his heart started to beat again. "That," he called, "is why I don't like swimming!"

Kat began to laugh. The crocodile stopped trying to climb the support and swam around it, opening and closing its mouth.

"At least it'll be easy to tie off the rope securely," she said, still grinning. "Then you can cross safely enough."

"Only after the crocodile leaves," said Andor. Mangos had forgotten all about him. "I'm not crossing until it leaves."

Nothing remained of the main gates of Terzol City but blackened rubble. They had been contested beyond their destruction; even the form of gates and towers had been destroyed. A partially cleared path allowed the victorious attackers, and centuries later them, to pass.

The wall slithered up to the ruined gates. It would be easy to think it useless, shaded as it was by the trees that rose high above it. Or maybe it was that much of the wall had been reduced to rubble, or that time and weather had failed to erase the mark of fire. Yet the wall still served as a boundary, and in places it still had grandeur;

twelve yards high where it stood unbroken, banded in grey and purple stone. It must have been grand, Mangos thought as they passed into Terzol the city.

What war started in the city, the jungle finished. Trees grew around and through the structures. Their roots pushed apart walls and wrapped up buildings. Grasses sprouted in a thin layer of soil that partially covered the streets. All was peaceful in the shade of the tall trees.

"We have seen you safely to Terzol," Mangos said.

"There is no safety in Terzol," came a voice. They turned to see a man crouched on top of one of the pillars. "Even now."

Andor turned very pale. "Why are you here? I have done nothing."

"Nothing but steal from the Bursa," said the man.

"The Bursa?" Mangos demanded in shock. "You stole from the Bursa?" He had heard of him—merchant prince, king of thieves, the most powerful man in Alomar after the true Prince.

"No!" Andor exclaimed. "I didn't! Only a scroll. Worthless, not even in the records. It had fallen behind the paneling."

"Ah," the man mused. "The Bursa was right. He didn't know what you took, only that you must have taken something."

Andor closed his mouth, his eyes popping from his face as he realized he had just confessed.

"Nobody," said the man, now talking to Mangos and Kat, "quits the Bursa and hires bodyguards unless they have done something... wrong." He sprang off the pillar, landing lightly. With a sword in one hand and a long knife in the other, he advanced on Andor. "Now I will recover this scroll and set an example of you." Andor sank to his knees in fear.

Kat stepped forward. "We can't let you do that."

"We can't?" said Mangos. "He's a treacherous little bastard. We *should* have fed him to the crocodile."

Kat's eyes never left the assassin. "If we're that particular about clients, we'll have few."

"Admirable," said the man. "But do you know who I am?"

"I think so," replied Kat. "The Hand of Bursa, though I'd not thought to see you outside of Alomar."

"This took me further than I expected. Our little bird flew very far indeed. But the Bursa does not tolerate theft, no matter how small."

The Hand of Bursa moved, and Mangos blinked, for it seemed he had not moved so much as disappeared and reappeared next to Kat.

72

Steel clashed. Mangos blinked again, for he had not seen Kat draw her blades, but nonetheless she had two.

He drew his own sword but waited for an opening.

Kat and the Hand fought in style—fluid, graceful, their blades whispering when they met and slid. Neither seemed to have weight, and both used their feet as weapons. They locked blades; the Hand swept Kat's feet from under her, and they rolled together, long knives flashing.

Mangos stopped, unable to attack as they changed positions so quickly.

They both rose, each bleeding, Kat from a nick under her chin, the Hand from a cut on his arm.

"Almost had you there," the Hand said.

"Almost."

"My turn," said Mangos and jumped forward. The Hand met his attack with his sword, swung in with his knife. Mangos drew back and swung low, trying to use his sword's longer reach to his advantage. Again the Hand parried and drove in. Surprised, Mangos clubbed him with the hilt of his sword and kicked away. The Hand grunted and shook his head.

Kat moved in to engage the Hand, and the fight swirled away, past Andor who seemed rooted on his knees, staring at those who fought over his life.

"Faster," Mangos said aloud. He and Kat attacked, driving the Hand back. They could not hurt him, but they drove him away from Andor, back toward the jungle. He gave ground, further, further back. He seemed a touch slower, perhaps still feeling Mangos's blow. A couple more exchanges, Mangos thought, and we'll have him.

The Hand dove and rolled, and attacked Mangos. Mangos gave a step, and the Hand was past him.

"No!" shouted Kat, but she bumped into Mangos, and the Hand was between them and Andor.

Andor looked up, eyes wide, hands at his side as the Hand leapt over him. He lifted his head to watch, and the Hand slashed down, slicing his neck. Blood showered the paving stones. He fell backwards, landing on his pack with a heavy thud, and then rolled onto his side where he twitched as blood spurted from his neck.

Kat and Mangos stopped. There was nothing they could do now.

The Hand stood over Andor. "No need to fight now? Good." He cut the straps on Andor's pack and flipped open the flap with his

73

knife. His eyes did not leave Kat and Mangos as he rummaged through the pack until he found what he wanted. He pulled out the brass tube, now crushed by Andor falling on it.

"He *was* a bastard," Kat said.

Prying off the top, the Hand looked in. He started to laugh. "Ironic." He poured flakes and dust from the flattened tube – all that remained of the receipt. "Did he ever tell you what he sought?"

"No," Mangos answered. Kat shook her head.

"No, he probably didn't. He's not going to steal from Bursa and share with you." He dropped the tube. It bounced twice and came to rest in Andor's blood. "You can take your pay from his body." He bent to wipe his blade on Andor's shirt and slid it back into its sheath. "Terzol has been picked clean for centuries. He should have known it wasn't worth the risk."

"Not if the Bursa would send you halfway across the world to protect his reputation," Kat remarked, a hint of irony in her voice.

"Just so," said the Hand, inclining his head as he accepted the compliment. "Good day. And good day it is, for you live to see the end of it." He turned to leave but paused. "Andor chose well for bodyguards, but early, I think. Time. With time and experience, you will be formidable." He nodded before disappearing into the jungle.

Mangos let out his breath with a loud 'whoosh.' "That didn't go well."

"I don't like failing in a commission," said Kat.

"We can hardly be blamed, by the gods of Eastwarn! The Hand of Bursa!" He nudged Andor with his foot. "You made powerful enemies."

"Shall we see why?" Kat raised an eyebrow.

Andor never told them where they went, but that didn't mean they didn't know. Mangos started to chuckle. He pulled the chain from around Andor's dead neck and tossed it to Kat. "We shall."

The square could hold thousands, tens of thousands. Mangos couldn't even imagine how many people it would take to pack such a place. The jungle had taken the city and invaded the buildings to either side, but the palace remained untouched. A dozen leopard statues flanked the broad steps to the portico, steps that rose fifty feet to columns that rose fifty more.

Wide terraces surrounded each level so that each was smaller than the one below and the whole building formed a pyramid. At the top, seemingly brushing the clouds, was the broken and vacant home of the god-emperors.

The emptiness made Terzol seem even larger, grander—too large for people.

Kat climbed the broad stone steps. The leopards looked down at her. Leopards, Mangos realized, who had looked down on the pageantry of emperors and treachery of generals. Leopards who had seen the wealth of an empire and the silence of centuries.

Kat wore that grandeur and sadness like a crown, as if she understood it and it was part of her. For a moment she was the Queen of a desolate country. Mangos shook his head to clear the image.

It took a day of searching through dark corridors that still stank of old fire and death, listening to their footsteps echo in empty halls, and picking through broken statues and the last rotting remains of furnishings. Finally, they stood outside a metal door leaning against its frame, one hinge broken and the other twisted by the door's weight. Kat ran her hand down the dented surface. "Here," she said, pausing to rub over a word barely discernable beneath a layer of red rust. "Mercantile vault."

She bent to pick up a battered lantern, lit it, and set it in an oddly-shaped mirrored box. Light bounced around the room, striking other mirrors and reflecting back and forth to illuminate a long chamber.

Broken pottery and chests littered the floor. Here and there a statue, masterfully carved, lay in pieces. Four heavy pillars obscured their view.

As they entered, their feet crushed shards of mirrors, broken glass from plates and vases, and shattered bones.

"It's been looted." Mangos stopped, looked and saw shadows on the far wall. "There."

They found six small vaults, each with a leopard's head snarling, black steel and cold, on the door. Four doors, a handspan thick and contoured to match the frame of the vault, were open. The vaults were empty.

Mangos squatted down to look at the lower of the two closed doors. "There is no keyhole." He reached inside the leopard's mouth. A faint noise, a creak of old metal, and he snatched his hand back just as the leopard bit down. The metal jaws clashed and relaxed, returning to their original position.

"That could—" He stopped as a thought crossed his mind. He peered under the metal fangs. Small holes in each. "Poison. Likely dried up, but you never know."

"Here," Kat said, handing him Andor's seal.

"Thanks," said Mangos. In the back of the leopard's mouth he could see an impression. It did not match the seal. "What if it belongs to a vault that's already open?"

Kat did not answer, and Mangos moved over to the other closed vault. The seal and impression matched. He grinned and then sobered as he lifted the seal near the leopard's mouth. "I really hope this works."

He pressed the seal into the back of the leopard's mouth. They could hear the sound of weights and counterweights tripping within the wall. Somewhere stone slid on stone.

The door swung open. The vault was a hollow in the wall four feet deep. Pushed to the back was a small leather bag, nicely filled.

All they need do was reach past a hole, as wide as the hollow and equally long, but of a depth Mangos could not tell. He wiggled his fingers and reached toward the hole.

"That would be foolish," Kat said.

There came a heavy rasping sound, as if called by Kat's words, and Mangos drew back is hand. The sound grew louder, and he could tell it came from the hole in the vault. A blunt nose appeared, poking up, and long tongue flicked out. A snake pushed up, out, and seemed to flow from the vault.

Mangos and Kat leapt back and drew their swords. The snake was pale green and yellow, and Mangos could not tell its length yet but he judged its width to be two feet. The snake lifted its head, fully as large as Mangos's. Its tongue flicked out as if tasting his smell on the air.

"I wouldn't count on its poison having dried up," said Kat.

It turned toward her voice and the light shone on its cloudy eyes. It flicked its tongue out. They could see more than twenty feet of snake and still it pulled itself out of the vault.

It struck.

Kat twisted as the snake shot by, curved, and she jumped to avoid its coils. She landed on its back, tumbled off and rolled, the snake striking just behind her.

"Why doesn't anything attack you first?" she complained. The snake struck again.

Mangos reversed his grip on his sword and plunged it into the snake. It thrashed, ripping the sword from his grip. Red blood welled around the sword and ran down its scales.

The snake raced away, taking Mangos's sword with it. He drew his long knife and drove it into the snake, edge toward its back. Bracing himself, he let the snake cut itself open as it rushed past. His teeth rattled as the knife bounced along the snake's ribs.

The tail whipped around, jarring him and knocking him back. It caught him again and knocked him over. Before he could rise a coil flopped on top of him. His breath left him but he struggled to free himself as the snake coursed over him.

It thrashed again; he didn't know what Kat did, but he rolled free. He knew he needed to get to the head. He couldn't kill the snake by beating its tail.

With a crash of broken glass, the room dimmed. The snake had knocked over several of the mirrors that lit the room. It reared its head and paused.

Silence. Mangos moved and it turned toward him.

"Make no noise," said Kat, hidden from view. "It's blind!"

The snake turned and struck at her voice. It vanished behind a pillar, and when it drew back, Kat was riding it, clinging just behind its head. She drew back her sword, thrust at its eye as it whipped back and forth. She missed, lost her grip and flew off, the snake after her before she struck the floor.

It scooped her in its coils, lifted her and opened its mouth to strike or eat.

Mangos grabbed its head. "If you let me attack first, this wouldn't happen," he grunted as he pulled back, his muscles straining. Kat couldn't answer, her face was red and arms were pinned to her body.

Mangos slipped down the snake, reached up, and grabbed a fang; it felt smooth and cool in his hand as he pulled himself up. He reached around with his knife and slid it into the snake's eye.

The snake went berserk and threw him off as it became a frenzied mass of coils. He pulled Kat free and they stumbled across the room to watch the snake convulse and die.

Kat lay against the wall and stretched her legs out in front of her, panting. Her hair stuck to her sweaty face. She closed her eyes. "I'll be fine," she said. "Just need to get my breath back."

When the snake no more than twitched, Mangos returned to the vault, stretched his hand all the way to the back, and drew out the pouch. He carried it back to Kat, sat on the ground beside her and worried at the drawstrings. He tipped it over and shook eight large gems out onto the dirty floor.

Leopard eye emeralds—so pure it looked like the green elliptical inclusion floated. Legends said they were formed by moonbeams captured when the world was formed. Mangos felt himself smiling like a fool. Kat stared at the emeralds spread before her like a fortune-teller trying to read the future in the bones.

"I think," said Mangos, "I'll sell mine. I can live like a king, drinking Ambraisen wine in the most pleasurable company. And I'll have a sword made, a hand-and-a-half sword with one of the emeralds set in the hilt." He stretched, enjoying fantasizing. "And I'll buy a copy of Teritum's *History of Terzol*."

Kat reached out to place a finger on a gem. She moved it aside and another that matched it exactly. "These two will be made into earrings. This one," she moved a larger stone next to the first two "will make a necklace."

"What of that one?" Mangos said, indicating the last emerald.

"This one," she rested her finger on her last stone and gently pushed it away from her, "will help buy an army."

79

# The Burning Fish

*Ten months after the fall of Alness.*

"This isn't the Burning Fish we need," Kat said.

"I know that!" Mangos retorted as he tried to push the fish off the hot stone. Smoke curled up, and the fish turned blacker and blacker. Finally, he drew his sword, slipped it under the fish, and flipped it onto a wooden plate.

Kat stood next to him, looking down at their burnt dinner. "I'd rather not be poisoned on this quest."

"If the worst thing that happens is our lunch, I'll be happy," Mangos said. But he laughed; there was nothing else he could do. "I turn my back for a minute..." He shook his head. Kat had been tending the mule that carried their gear and the special barrel that would let them transport a Burning Fish once they found one.

Baron Endelhorn wanted a Burning Fish because it was his family's crest, and he was willing to pay very generously for one. The true Burning Fish would burst into flames when it leapt from the water only to be extinguished when it fell back in. It was, Mangos had always thought, legendary, but after rummaging through old records in the ruins of Terzol, Kat said they might be able to find one.

"I thought I would save time," Mangos gestured to the well-stoked fire, prodding the plate with his foot. He would have to be starving before he tried to eat that fish.

"It was said the right sized fish would cook itself perfectly if it wasn't returned to the water," Kat said.

"Then the fish could cook itself better than I can cook it." He sighed. "How much further to the lake?"

Kat shot him a look that seemed to say, *if you learned to read, you would know this for yourself.*

Mangos threw dirt over the fire and took up the mule's halter. The journey was easy—plentiful fish and game, and pleasant shade under the forest canopy. It was almost like being paid for a pleasure trip.

Best to enjoy things while they were good.

Yellow flowers dotted the forest floor. They looked like little suns, globes of tightly bunched petals just starting to open. Their sweet smell tickled his nose and made the forest seem cheerful.

Presently he caught a glimpse of the lake far ahead, sunlight sparkling off its surface. They emerged from the trees on the east shore. The lake was half a mile across, and something more than that in length. They were closer to the south end of the lake than the north.

Grey stone buildings clustered at the north end, an enduring reminder of the former power and reach of Terzol. Vines crawled over half the buildings, and empty darkness gaped through their windows and doors. The rest had been cleared of growth and fitted with shutters and doors of rough-hewn wood to keep out the weather.

Made small by the distance, people moved around the buildings and on the beach. A few used large baskets to fish while others worked on the beach.

Mangos shaded his eyes, trying to see more clearly. "There are people here."

"People?" Kat came up behind him. "What kind of people? The only people in these mountains are hunters."

"Just people."

"They're not from the Terzol valley, and it looks like they're fishing for food, not trade."

"They must be crazy. This is nowhere. Go to Alomar, people," he growled. "You can *buy* fish in Alomar."

"Not Burning Fish," Kat remarked, her tone thoughtful.

An old man sat on the sandy beach, watching the fishers. Another man sat next to him, weaving a fishing basket. Several more people moved around, some carrying wood or fresh cut rushes. They all stopped working as Mangos and Kat approached.

"Are you pilgrims?" one of the fishing women asked. She was only a year or two older than Mangos, brown hair bleached by the sun, wearing a tunic that came to her knees, the bottom inch wet from the waves.

*Pilgrims?* Mangos wondered. "No," he said.

"Who are you?" Kat asked the group.

They turned to the old man to answer. He bowed his head in respectful greeting before saying, "We serve Tourlan, the goddess of the lake."

There was a stone table with a roughly carved wooden fish on it halfway up the beach. *That's a pretty poor altar,* Mangos thought. Did they expect pilgrims for that?

"Tourlan?" Kat raised an eyebrow. She appeared thoughtful. "You are far from civilization."

"We are. Yet the goddess is here, so here we serve."

"We won't bother you," assured Mangos. "We'll just get what we need and leave you to your goddess."

"What do you need?"

"A Burning Fish."

The crowd murmured and an angry, wordless grumble came from many throats. The old man's eyes widened a fraction, he glanced at his followers, and licked his lips. "The Burning Fish are sacred to Tourlan," he said. "You may not disturb them."

"The Terzoli served them for dinner," Kat remarked. She jerked her head around to encompass the village. Mangos wondered if these people even knew the origin of the buildings.

"And look what happened to Terzol," the old man retorted.

"You think there's a connection?" Kat asked.

The old man took his gaze from the buildings and turned it on her. "Yes."

"You eat fish," Mangos protested, pointing at the women fishing.

"Not the goddess's sacred fish," the old man replied.

"It's fortunate nobody wants to eat one," Kat said. "The earl wants one because it's the symbol of his family. It would be honored."

The woman who first spoke opened her mouth, her expression angry. The old man forestalled her by shaking his head and saying, "No."

The man weaving fish traps reached for a rusty sword lying beside him. "Darnow," the old man said. "That isn't necessary. They have traveled a long way. They may rest here before returning home."

Darnow glanced at the women in the water before drawing back his hand. He didn't say anything but still glared.

"Tourlan has given us more than we need." The old man gestured at the stone buildings. "You are welcome to use one." He looked coy as he said, "Maybe you'd like to learn more of our goddess."

Mangos ducked his head as he entered the small building. The thick slates forming the roof remained solid, successfully protecting the massive timbers that supported them. The heavy cut stones of the walls remained straight and true. Leaves gathered in the corners, but somebody had swept most of them out so it looked like autumn on the ground outside. An old blanket hung over the door.

"I don't think he's letting us stay from any feeling of charity,"

Mangos said. "He just wants to keep an eye on us."

"There are four people who matter," Kat said with a nod. "The High Priest, of course, and the old woman who sat next to him. She didn't talk, but she also didn't work, so she has some influence. The girl who was fishing in the water—she wants to be the new leader, you can tell by how she acts. The man weaving fish traps is the other. I don't know how smart he is, but he's clearly willing to fight. The rest are sheep."

Mangos scratched the back of his neck. "I'm willing to bet any of them could get a Burning Fish pretty easily. Maybe somebody will quietly sell us one."

"Can't hurt to try," Kat said. "Except the trap weaver is a fighter. A tough and dirty fighter, if I had to guess."

Mangos thought of the villagers. The High Priest was Barnor, and though he tried to hide it, his left leg was horribly scarred. The woman who stayed near him was Saralyn. The young woman was Danielse. As Kat said, Darnow was a scarred fighter, younger than Barnor, but still older and more experienced than Mangos. There were more who kept to the back. Barely individuals, together they gave strength to Barnor's refusal.

"There's a stream flowing from the east side of the lake," Kat noted. "It might be a good place to trap fish."

"I'll try to get a Burning Fish the easy way."

"Cooking it?"

Mangos laughed. "Getting one from those who know best."

*I*'*ll start with these two*, Mangos thought.

Saralyn crouched at the water's edge, washing reeds.

Danielse carried a bundle of yellow flowers to the altar. Bowing her head, she arranged them around the fish carving. Dropping to her knees, she bowed her head again before brushing the sand smooth.

She rose and came to the edge of the water, humming a tune that wandered like a lost adventurer—going nowhere, but happy about it. She sat, putting her feet in the lake, and began to braid the flowers in her hair.

Saralyn frowned at her but didn't say anything. Danielse kept braiding while the older woman worked.

"Have you seen a Burning Fish?" Mangos asked.

"They're beautiful," Danielse said. "They leap high out of the water and burst into blue flame." She sighed, enraptured by her memory. "So lovely. The goddess favors me," she added.

Saralyn rolled her eyes. "So you keep reminding us."

"You saw one?" Mangos prompted.

"My first day," Danielse replied. Her smile was vacant, as if the past was still before her. "The spring rains had flooded my family's farm and drowned my parents. I tried to reach town, but I got turned around avoiding the floods and wandered until I ended up here. The goddess welcomed me with the sight of Burning Fish." She blinked herself back to the present and returned to braiding the flowers into her hair.

*She's not going to give us one*, Mangos thought. *The Fish are too holy.* He turned to Saralyn. "Have you seen one?"

Saralyn pursed her lips. "No."

"She cleaned the High Priest's house for years without the goddess revealing her sacred text," Danielse said.

"Don't sound so smug." Saralyn glared. "You can't read it. Nobody can."

"A text?" Mangos felt he was in the middle of an old argument and didn't know half the terms.

"A worthless old book," Saralyn spat.

"A sacred book," Danielse insisted. "It's written in the goddess's sacred script."

"So you claim!" Sarilyn retorted. "By the goddess, your foolishness makes me ill!"

"You," Mangos hesitated to suggest, "could leave?"

"Leave? Where would I go? Beyond fishing, I have no woodcraft. Besides, except for *her*, it's not so bad. Quiet. And I have a certain influence with Barnor." She smiled a prim smile at Danielse.

"What she means is she's a slave and can't leave," Danielse said.

Saralyn gasped. "It doesn't matter here," she snapped. "My life is no different from anybody else's."

Danielse smirked.

"*You* could leave," Saralyn said. Her tone betrayed her eagerness.

Danielse looked incredulous. "Go out in the world? Serve a baron or an earl? Why? Here I serve a *goddess!*"

*This isn't helping*, Mangos thought. *Danielse won't give a Fish, and it's clear Saralyn never leaves the village.*

At the edge of the trees, Darnow lurked. He caught Mangos's eye and motioned him over. Mangos gladly excused himself and trudged up the beach.

Darnow looked around. "How much will you pay for one?" he whispered.

Mangos looked up. Darnow could only be talking about a Burning Fish. *How much would we pay for one?* Mangos wondered. *Better yet, does he truly have one to sell?* It seemed too easy.

Darnow drew him closer, as a conspirator would. Mangos could smell smoke and sweat and rotting teeth. "How much?" Darnow repeated.

"You have one to sell?" Mangos asked.

Darnow scratched behind an ear, drew his hand down and pulled at his upper lip. "Course I have."

"And you're willing to sell the goddess's sacred fish?"

Darnow turned his head and spat in the sand. "If your gold is good."

*He doesn't think much of the goddess,* Mangos thought. *But he thinks a lot of that fish.* He wondered why Darnow needed gold. He couldn't spend it here. "You think a fish is worth gold?"

"You think a fish is worth coming all the way out here." Darnow smiled, showing not just his rotting teeth but several gaps. "Think about it." He stood, evidently having noticed Danielse fishing, and puffed out his chest before walking away.

"So," said Kat.

Mangos jumped, spun, and glared. He hadn't known she was sitting on the other side of the tree.

"Darnow is planning on leaving sometime," she continued. "And my guess is he wants to take Danielse with him." She snorted, a sound of skepticism. "He'll need luck and a new set of teeth for that."

"But he can get us a fish," Mangos mused.

"Can he? He might sell us a fish, or he might murder us in our sleep. I wouldn't bet either way."

They told each other what they had discovered. Kat went first, telling him there would be no fish in the outflow stream. The water level was too low.

Mangos told her of Saralyn and Danielse's argument, and she agreed there was little more to be gained there, though the book interested her.

"And," she said, "we need to talk to Barnor. Alone would be best."

They didn't get a chance until late afternoon when the beach was empty and Barnor was limping alone to the altar. He took out a rag and began to wipe the top.

"I'd like to talk to you about the goddess," Kat said quietly.

Barnor looked at her from the sides of his eyes then glanced over at Mangos. He repositioned his scarred leg to make it more comfortable. "Talk."

"Tourlan was a prostitute in Denoit, famous because she could—" Kat cleared her throat. "Never mind why she was famous. She might still be alive, but she'd be old, and certainly not a goddess. Also, the Terzoli harvested Burning Fish for generations and never mentioned deities. Strange that one should suddenly settle in now."

*Ha,* Mangos thought, *the whole thing is a sham.*

"I spent my whole life in these mountains," Barnor said. "When I was a lad, a few old men hunted here, but they died, and I was the only one. I got tired of it, lonely if you will. I was starting to look for something else when I ruined my leg." He slapped his scarred leg. "Hard to go anywhere then, worse now."

"Live somewhere else," Mangos said.

Barnor shook his head. "Maybe you would, maybe you bend to the world, but I bend the world to me. I knew about this village, of course, and of the Burning Fish."

Kat leaned back, smiling. She nodded. She must have guessed Barnor's story.

Barnor wadded up the rag and resumed wiping off the top of the altar. Mangos suddenly realized this was not really an altar, just a stone table once used for cleaning fish. It had a groove around the edge and a hole in one end to wash down the scales and offal. He couldn't suppress a snort of amusement, wondering how many of the goddess's sacred fish had been cleaned on her altar.

"So," Barnor said, continuing his story, "I made up the story of Tourlan, the goddess of the lake. I became High Priest and went out to recruit acolytes." He grinned, eyes twinkling. "The original Tourlan was something of a goddess, too, at least when I was a young man."

"And people fell for it," Mangos said, half a statement, half a question, for it seemed incredible, yet there they were.

Barnor snorted and smiled like a boy caught in a clever lie. "I had to buy my first follower because nobody would join. After that it was easier."

"Then it shouldn't be a problem for us to take a fish," Mangos said.

Barnor shook his head. "The High Priest loses face if he gives away the goddess's sacred fish."

"Nobody need know," said Kat.

"You still can't have one," Barnor shook his head again, "because there aren't any left."

The water lay flat, untroubled by wind or wave. A faint mist hovered over the surface. A large bird, a heron, glided down, wings not moving, coasting on the air until it nearly touched the water. It dropped its legs, flapped, and came to a stop standing in the center of concentric circles that rushed away from it. Further away, a fish jumped. A normal fish.

According to Barnor, it was four years since any there had seen a Burning Fish, and Mangos believed him. After confessing to making up the religion, Barnor had nothing to gain by lying about the fish.

*How could Darnow sell us a Burning Fish if there aren't any?* Mangos wondered as he leaned on the windowsill. Dusk was fast approaching. *What does he know?*

Kat came into the building, walked right to the lamp and sat beside it. She pulled a medium-sized book from under her cloak and opened it.

"You stole the goddess's book!" Mangos exclaimed.

"Quiet," Kat whispered forcefully. "I'm pretty sure the goddess can't hear you, but let's not take our chances with the others."

"Nobody can read the book," Mangos reminded her.

"That," Kat said, "is because they can't read Terzoli."

Mangos blinked, caught off guard. "Terzoli?"

"This is just a Terzoli log book. I told you they served Burning Fish at the Emperor's banquets and they built this village to supply the fish." She ran her finger down the first page.

"But—" Mangos started.

"It's the same thing we're doing," Kat explained. "They just had a system to do it regularly." She fell silent as she read. After a minute, she said, "And to ensure a predictable supply of fish."

"Well, it'd be embarrassing if the Emperor didn't have Burning Fish to eat."

"And therefore unacceptable." Kat turned the page, grimaced. "Some fool didn't mix the ink right. Look at this," she pointed half way down the page, where the words seemed to vanish. "It's so faded you can't read it." She flipped several more pages until coming to one with writing. "Ah, better. New ink, mixed properly this time."

"There is another lake," she said after studying the page for a moment. She looked over toward the window. "It must be on the west side because it flows into this one."

Mangos went to the window and looked west, where the mountains were further from the shore, looking for a break in the trees. He couldn't see anything in the dusk, so he turned his attention back to the book on the table.

Kat turned the page and groaned. "They let that idiot make ink again." She started to flip pages. Nothing.

"What can it tell us?" Mangos asked.

"Not enough. There was something important about the other lake. There were no Burning Fish in it, but the Terzoli did something, something they felt would allow them to control the harvest of Burning Fish."

"And?" Mangos prompted.

"And they ran out of ink. Finished the entry in a new batch, and it faded to nothing."

Mangos found a break in the trees in a small cove. A shelf of rock sloped down to the lake. There was a hole in its flat surface about forty feet from shore. A pile of wilted flowers and a small cup of water sat next to the hole.

"Home of the goddess, I expect," Mangos murmured as he surveyed the offering.

He could see the upper lake while standing next to the hole. Its surface was three or four feet higher than the lower lake, the water held back by a natural dam of stone packed with branches and leaves, held in place by grass and small shrubs.

Mangos walked up the shelf of grey slate. Water trickled over the dam, making a river an inch deep and narrow enough to step over. The river vanished into the "goddess's home."

The Burning Fish never appeared in the upper lake, yet the Terzoli fish keepers felt the lake important, and required great care.

He climbed onto the dam.

The upper lake was deep. He didn't want to judge, knowing how water could distort distances, but it was at least ten feet deep near the sides, and in the center the bottom plunged out of sight.

Curious.

He just didn't know why it was curious.

He walked off the dam, brushed his feet through the leaves on the forest floor. He wasn't good at puzzles. Adventures were supposed to be about fighting and drinking and treasures and pleasant company.

He sighed. What was the connection between the upper and lower lakes? A pittance of a stream too small for fish.

But there were no Burning Fish.

Maybe, Mangos thought, there are no fish because there is no connection.

Walking back onto the dam, he realized he had only thought it natural. Under all the grass and dirt, the stones had been fitted together.

Curious.

He crouched down, pulled up some grass, and ran his hand over the mortared stones. There was no doubt. Should he get Kat?

He jumped off the dam and walked down to the goddess's home. Cool air and darkness rose from it. He could hear water dripping. Home of the goddess or work of the Terzoli? He crouched down to see better.

The wind stirred. Mangos felt it on his back. It blew through the forest and brought with it the smell of flowers.

Something very hard struck him on the back of his head, and he pitched into the hole.

M angos opened his eyes. A dozen halos of light danced above him, slowly revolving down to one. The light felt painful. He shivered. He was cold. His muscles felt tight and his head pounded, but nothing worse. Lucky.

He sat up and felt water run from his hair, heard it drip. He was sitting in three inches of water on another slate shelf. Luckily, he had been lying face up, or he would have drowned.

He reached up and touched his head. His hand came away wet, but not bloody. Lucky again. A man had no right to expect such luck.

He was at the end of a cavern, the area around him lit by the hole above, the rest melding to darkness to his left. Water fell through the sunlight, like diamonds into darkness to splash beside him as mere water again.

A few feet away the rock shelf ended, the pool suddenly dark, and Mangos had no idea how deep it might be.

Branches and bones wedged in the rock wall showed the water had been higher in the past. Some sort of plant grew from cracks in the wall. It looked like kelp, with long vines and narrow leaves, and it trailed in the water.

As his eyes adjusted, he could see the further walls. Walls, he realized, that separated him from the two lakes on either side. He hoped they were thick.

A large fish swam up and nibbled a trailing plant. After a few bites, it swam away, but there were dozens more, appearing and disappearing in the dark water.

Mangos picked up a plant; it felt warm to his touch. He rolled it between his fingers, crushing the leaves. Heat flared on his fingertips.

There was a splash. Mangos saw a twinkle of light out of the corner of his eye. When he turned his head, all he saw were small waves rushing from where a fish had jumped.

Then another. The fish hung over the water, longer than he would have suspected, and he saw it clearly illuminated by blue flames. Then it splashed back into the pool, and the flames vanished.

*Burning Fish!* He scrambled to his feet.

The fish darted away, but he didn't care. He had found them!

His stomach growled. He didn't worry about starving, though. Not with all the fish around just waiting to cook themselves. He was more concerned with getting out. He had no idea how.

The hole was twenty-five feet up, high enough that he considered himself lucky not to have been injured when falling, but far too high to reach. The ceiling overhung the walls. He might climb the walls, but he couldn't stretch far enough to reach the hole.

He gave up trying and searched for some way to catch a fish. A shadow fell on the floor. Mangos looked up.

Kat leaned over the opening, her hair hanging down.

"Get me out!" Mangos called. "I found the Burning Fish." He told her of the fish, and the plants, and the inability to climb out.

A rope snaked down and splashed in the water. "Why did you climb down if you can't get back out?"

Mangos grabbed the rope and pulled himself up. "I didn't." He tilted his head as if she could see the bruise through his hair. "Somebody knocked me in."

That wiped the grin from her face. "Who?"

"I didn't see them."

Kat turned toward the village, as if she could tell Mangos's attacker just by looking. "Did they think the fall would kill you, or that I wouldn't be able to find you?"

"I don't know," Mangos replied. "They likely believed the fall would kill me."

"Then it's decision time," Kat said. Mangos looked at her in surprise. "We can grab a couple fish and take them to the Baron. Or we find who attacked you and sink them in the lake."

"That one." Mangos rubbed his head meaningfully. "We can get the fish afterwards."

Kat nodded.

Mangos felt, and heard, his stomach rumble again.

With a laugh, Kat dug into her pack and pulled out a small loaf of bread and some fish. "I got some dried fish from the village." She held up the food, but seemed distracted, perhaps her mind on the attack.

Mangos reached for the bread. Kat gave it to him and took the fish for herself.

"To the fish," Mangos toasted. They saluted each other with the food and took a bite.

Kat swallowed. She looked into the cavern. "Let's assume it's a combination of a particular type of fish eating the special plants that only grow in the cavern."

"If the cavern floods, some of the fish can escape," Mangos said. "Maybe without the dam it's always flooded."

Kat nodded. "That makes sense. And if the fish swim freely in the lake, they eat other things besides the right plant. By keeping the fish in the cavern, the Terzoi made it easy for themselves."

Mangos waved aside the conversation. "I only want two things," he said. "Find whoever pushed me and get a Burning Fish back to the Baron."

"If we can't figure who pushed you, I'm inclined to take the fish and leave." Kat grinned, her expression feral. "Or we can kill them all."

Suddenly she gagged, swallowed and gagged again. Her eyes went wide, and she stared in horror at the fish in her hand. She threw it out into the lake and immediately began to cough.

"What's wrong?" Mangos asked.

She could not answer, she was coughing too hard, looking to be on the verge of throwing up. She doubled over, clutching at her stomach.

Mangos didn't know what to do; something was very wrong. "Poison?" he asked, dropping his bread.

She nodded her head in jerky motions, slumped over, struggling to breathe.

"What can I do?"

Kat gagged and coughed. A trickle of blood leaked from the corner of her mouth.

Mangos scooped her up, lifted her over his shoulder. He started to walk, then jog, then run back to the village as Kat's coughing eased and she went limp.

"Don't die," he told her, "don't die."

Barnor was sitting next to the lake with the others gathered around him when Mangos reached the village.

"What happened?" Barnor asked.

Danielse and Darnow craned their heads, looking curious, then alarmed. "What bit her?" Darnow asked.

"Nothing bit her, she's been poisoned," Mangos said. "Help her!"

"Poisoned?" Saralyn leaned over to examine Kat. "She knows better than to eat unknown berries and roots."

"Somebody gave her poisoned fish. Somebody here."

Mangos slid Kat off his shoulder, set her down, and laid her back. Her skin felt cold. Her face was white, giving the streak of blood a ghastly appearance. Her eyes were closed, but her eyelids spasmed.

"Help her!" Mangos commanded. It felt like Kat was slipping away and nobody felt any urgency. "If she dies, I'll kill everybody here."

Darnow glared, clapped his hand to his sword and stepped forward, the stink of him filling the air. But Mangos eagerly reached for his own sword. It might not save Kat, but killing Darnow would be doing *something*.

"Draw that sword, and I'll turn the altar back to its original purpose," Mangos growled. "But it's you I'll fillet."

"Please," Saralyn interjected. "It's not that easy." She shook her head. "I don't know antidotes." She looked at the others.

"I do," Barnor said. "But I need to know what she ate."

Mangos glared at the small crowd. The poisoner knew what they used. Who was it?

Barnor? He was a liar and a fraud. If they took a Burning Fish after he denied them one, it would make him look weak. He could be pretending not to know.

What of Darnow? He could be angry they wouldn't pay him and afraid they would reveal his attempt to sell a fish.

Saralyn? Maybe she feared the group would disband if Barnor were to look weak. She could have done it without Barnor knowing about it.

Kat convulsed, then lay still. She would die soon.

Any of them could have poisoned her.

It would be the same person that knocked him into the cavern, he realized. They didn't expect Kat to find him because they thought she would be dead.

A breeze stirred the smell of fish and ash and fresh cut pine, and another smell he recognized…

"What did you use to poison Kat?" Mangos demanded.

Danielse shrank back. "Nothing! What makes you think I did anything?"

"Anybody could have poisoned Kat," he said, "but you're the one who knocked me into the pit." He curled his lip in contempt. "Barnor cannot walk that far. Saralyn doesn't leave the village—and Darnow? I'd have smelled Darnow. Instead, I smelled flowers."

Danielse clutched at her hair, let her hand drop, pulling one of the flowers with it. She lifted her chin. "You will not steal Tourlan's sacred fish."

"Damn the fish! What poison did you use? If she dies, you die."

"Then I will be a martyr for the goddess."

Mangos grabbed the flower from her and brandished it at Barnor. "She uses these for everything. Are they poisonous?"

"Yes."

Danielse glared, and Mangos knew it was true. "Can you cure Kat?" he asked.

Barnor nodded. "I think so. Aanerberry juice should do it."

"Let her die!" shrieked Danielse. "She would defame the goddess! Tell them," she implored Barnor. "Tell them it is true."

"I—I," Barnor faltered.

Mangos sheathed his sword. "Don't waste my time, and don't waste Kat's."

66 "She's coming around." Mangos nodded to Saralyn, who came to sit next to Kat. The old woman readied a glass of water.

Kat opened her eyes. She seemed dazed as she looked around. She focused on Mangos and said, "There's something I need to do."

Saralyn gave her the water. "Drink. You need to drink."

"No," said Kat, "that's not it."

"You need to feel better. It will take some time," Saralyn said.

"What will make me feel better won't take long at all," Kat answered, pushing herself up. She wobbled a little and didn't look any steadier as she made her way to the door. She put her hand on the frame and paused, breathing heavily.

"You need to rest. The poison damaged your stomach."

Kat ignored her. "You'll want to come," she told Mangos. "She tried to kill you too."

Mangos nodded, he did want to come, but he opened his mouth to protest. He meant to say Kat should rest, but the look in her eyes and his own desire for revenge changed his mind. "I don't know where she is."

"What are you going to do?" Saralyn sounded both fearful and resigned.

Kat again ignored her. She walked to the beach, slowly, clearly concentrating on her movement. Barnor sat on the sand. He didn't say anything, nor did he try to stop her.

Danielse was not on the beach or in the water.

Kat brushed the wilted flowers off the altar as she walked toward the water's edge and around the west shore of the lake.

"Where's Darnow?" she asked.

"Gone," called Barnor from behind them.

"I wonder what he took," Kat said, but kept walking.

Realizing she headed toward the "goddess's home," Mangos moved ahead of her. His heart beat faster as he neared, expecting to see Danielse kneeling beside the hole in the rock.

It was empty except for a scattering of yellow flowers.

"She's not here," he said as Kat approached. He looked down. Something caught his eye.

He crouched at the hole and stuck his head down, waiting a second for his eyes to adjust. Danielse lay, face down, in the shallow water. Jumped, fell, or pushed; drowned or broken, Mangos couldn't tell, but she was clearly dead.

He straightened up and motioned to Kat. She came over to look.

"She found refuge in the arms of the goddess," Kat said. "One way or another."

# Deathwater

*A tale of Maarkin, the Assassin.*

Across from Maarkin, Calex lifted his goblet of ginger wine. "To the passing of time and kings."

Maarkin lifted his own goblet, almost against his will. The amber liquid caught the evening sun and sparkled like a gemstone.

He hesitated, reluctant to drink.

Caresa's irritated glance echoed her earlier words about attending this private dinner; one does not refuse the invitations of kings. Drink.

*What do I fear?* He asked himself.

He knew he hadn't killed in years and he had no desire to do so now. Why else would a new king summon his assassin?

Jervis had been *amused* to have an assassin, because he never needed one. But Jervis was dead, and Calex was king. Untested, politically weak, and unpredictable.

Caresa cleared her throat, a tiny, angry sound. They were waiting for him to drink.

*I don't want to be an assassin,* he admitted. He liked the life he had and didn't want to kill anyone to keep it. But to live that life, he needed money, and working for Jervis had been perfect. *Well, I can always refuse if Calex asks.*

He had already eaten, he may as well drink. As Caresa said, what choice did he have?

He drank. The wine was excellent, just like the rest of dinner.

It wasn't just him. Times had changed. The Temple had a new Inquest to catch murderers—at least of the powerful. He didn't even know how it worked, just that the Goddess was involved and it couldn't be beaten. He didn't *want* to deal with it.

He set his goblet down amongst the crystal, silver, and leftovers of the consumed feast. Fish—not from the canals because everybody knew them to be too polluted. Spiced goat. Fresh bread. Last season's vegetables preserved and enhanced by magic. All this for a man whose noble blood was diluted by several generations and a woman with none at all.

"What do you want?" he demanded.

Caresa drew in her breath at his effrontery.

Calex rose and walked over to the railing of the terrace. With a jerk

96

of his head, he indicated they should follow.

The view was splendid. The city with all its canals lay spread out below them. The watermen with their orca-drawn carriages moved like water spiders across the surface. If he tried, Maarkin could pick out his house across the bay.

Calex rapped his knuckles on a small box, and, for the first time, Maarkin noticed the table in the shadow of the railing and the rosewood box on top of it.

"I want you to kill somebody for me," Calex said.

All the rich food felt heavy in Maarkin's stomach, but he temporized. "It's been a long time."

Calex curled his lip. He opened the box. Inside lay two phials of faintly luminous violet liquid.

"Oh," said Caresa in wonder. "What's that?"

"Antidote," Calex said.

*Damn!* Maarkin knew what that meant. *I should have listened to my fears!* He might have been paranoid, but he wasn't paranoid enough. He hadn't acted on it. "You thought I'd refuse," he said angrily.

"I can't let you refuse. And when you hear the target you may still try."

"You poisoned me!" Maarkin reached for the box.

Calex closed it. "This isn't the cure. Maybe antidote is too strong a word. Call it a 'reprieve.' Each dose will hold off the poison for twenty-four hours, that's all."

"Who?"

"The Duke of Savongy."

There wasn't a word formidable enough to describe that target. Savongy was protected by the new Inquest.

Caresa watched the two with wide eyes.

"Why?" Maarkin demanded. Savongy was well-liked. He had been critical of Calex for not being able to clean the canals, but that was just the loudest voice of many.

"You won't kill him for my reasons, so I'm not going to tell you," Calex said. "Kill him to save your own life."

"He's protected by the Inquest. My life is forfeit either way."

"Then do it for her."

"Who her?" Caresa said with a note of alarm.

"You," Maarkin snapped. "You poisoned her too?"

Caresa shook her head. "No, no, no."

Calex ignored her. "Yes, of course. The poison inside you was made

97

by Felkirk last month—just before he died. Nobody else knows how to make it. Sadly, all his notes and recipes were destroyed in the fire that killed him."

"How convenient." That meant Maarkin couldn't find the poison or the cure anywhere else. "Have you thought of becoming your own assassin?"

"Don't be stupid. Killing Felkirk wouldn't have taken any skill—if he was even killed. Accidents *do* happen." Calex folded his arms.

"You'll give me both cures if I escape the Inquest?"

"If *I* escape the Inquest."

Maarkin glared at him. "Two days isn't enough time under normal conditions, and I know nothing of the Inquest."

"Nothing to know," Calex said with a wave of his hand. "It can't be beaten. But," he made a show of checking the clock, "you have two days to do it."

"I need more time."

"There are several reasons you can't have it, but the only one that matters to you is—there's no more reprieve."

Maarkin took a deep breath, trying to calm himself. "If you give Caresa the cure, the reprieve will last twice as long. I *will* carry out your orders."

Calex lifted his hand, first finger up as if he were going to say something profound. "No." He dropped his hand. "The reprieve is what matters to you. It's not what matters to me. And," he indicated Caresa with a nod of his head, "I'm guessing you'll work hard to keep her alive. Maybe hard enough."

"I don't even know how quickly the Temple begins an Inquest, or how long one takes."

"They're quick. Trust me."

*Little chance of that.* But he had little choice either. He had to take the job believing he could, if not save himself, at least find a way to save Caresa. He turned to leave.

"Nobody walks out on the king," Calex said. He gave them a lazy smile. "But I forgive you." He pointed toward a covered chaffing dish. "More desert for me."

#### One hour since he had consumed the poison.

Caresa wept in the carriage as they crossed the bay. The waterman kept his face forward, toward his orcas, pretending he didn't

98

notice, for which Maarkin was grateful.

*I got soft*, he thought. He'd done so many stupid things; bought a home amongst the artists, collected rare manuscripts, mixed spices instead of poisons. He'd even taken a lover.

All the while he'd neglected his skills, letting both his knowledge and magic grow stale. *Calex must be desperate to tie his fate to mine.* At least he was still in shape, though more from vanity than necessity.

"I'm sorry," he murmured to Caresa. It wasn't his fault, but he was sorry she suffered for what he was.

*A poor excuse for an assassin.*

The waterman reined the orcas at the landing nearest his house. Maarkin helped Caresa from the carriage. The waterman's eyes lingered on her as she climbed the steps to the top of the quay.

It was a common reaction, enhanced by her dress. The first thing she had done upon moving in with Maarkin was buy a dress suitable for dining at the palace, one that was elegant and just shy of scandalous the way it dipped in front and revealed on the sides.

She adjusted it as she walked, a habit, for she reveled in attention. She loved the notoriety of being an assassin's girl.

Maarkin hadn't closed the door to his house before she wailed, "I don't want to die!"

"I know," he said.

"What are you going to do about it?"

*I'd be a fool to tell you.* Rumors said the Inquestor could track a quarrel back to the finger that pulled the crossbow's trigger. She could tell the truth from lies in both the living and the dead. It seemed unlikely that he could save himself, but he must keep Caresa as far from this job as possible.

"You need to find me a cure," she demanded.

He shook his head. "It would take too long, if I even could."

"*Buy* one, you idiot."

He hadn't used his skills as an assassin in so long she didn't even know what they were. "I'm a better poisoner than any apothecary in the city, but Felkirk was better still."

He opened one of the phials and smelled the reprieve within. It smelled of violets and peppermint. He knew this family of poisons; they were all subtle and deadly. Worse, while their antidotes shared some ingredients, what was necessary to cure one poison served to accelerate another.

Worse still, he had no reason to doubt Calex had used an entirely

99

new poison that was similar, but not identical to, an existing one.

He could not make his own cure. The most he could do was stretch out the poison, take the reprieve after twenty-eight hours and gain an extra four by doing so. The extra four hours would not be pleasant, but they might be necessary.

He realized Caresa was watching him. "We can't buy a cure," he said.

With an angry 'huff,' she went upstairs. He followed. She went straight to the nightstand, grabbing a glass of wine she had left that afternoon and finishing it in one go. She set the glass back down, using, he noticed with irritation, his arcane bloodstone as a coaster.

He was a fair mage, when it served his profession to be, but no magic could cure poison.

There was only one hope to save them. Maybe he could find a loophole in the Inquest's power. He would need to do some research to learn about the Inquest and how it worked. Then he could form a plan. He absolutely couldn't give Caresa any information that might be used against her.

"Do you have any place else to stay?" he asked.

"You're throwing me out?" She stared at him, incredulous. "I'm dying!"

*You know too much already*, he thought. *I can't even tell you what I can't tell you.* "I'm not throwing you out. I'm—it would better if—" *I don't have time for this. Not if you want to live.*

"If I didn't bother you with my dying?"

"I didn't say that. But maybe you're right. Maybe it would be best if you stayed here. But you can't see this."

He reached out to touch her neck. With the least amount of pressure, he sent her into unconsciousness. "I'll apologize when this is over." *Unless we're dead. Then it won't matter.*

*Focus.*

The city had two factions: the Landward one made of nobility whose holdings were in the country's interior and the Seaward nobles from the coastal areas. There was tension between the two, but the country flourished when they were balanced.

Savongy was a powerful Landward noble, but respected by both factions. He was forty-one, a fact Maarkin knew because last year on his fortieth birthday Savongy bought everybody in his district drinks. He didn't even check to see if they were residents or visitors.

*I don't want to kill a good man. I don't want to kill anybody at all.*

He couldn't let anybody know his interest in the Inquest or Savongy. So, a disguise.

He hurried to one of the bookcases and tripped the first catch on the bookcase, then the second. Finally, he moved the statue of the six-legged lizard—one more leg than a person has fingers on their hand—onto the six pressure plates and pulled the proper book to work the counterweights.

The bookcase swung open. Caresa didn't know about this room; he hadn't gotten *that* soft. Here he kept the tools of his trade, all that he needed for his magics and poisons. His weapons and disguises. His disguises...

Taller or shorter? Shorter. The thicker his soles the more difficult agility became. He slipped off his thick-soled boots and choose a pair with thinner soles.

He took off his glasses. He didn't need them anyway.

He hated the mustache, shaving it off was a pleasure. He selectively dyed some of his hair grey; it took too much time to make it look natural, but he couldn't afford half-measures.

A bit of putty here and there lengthened his nose and built up his cheekbones. Some balm tanned his skin. He wanted to look like he spent more time outside.

And now for his voice. He opened the cabinet to survey the dozens of small jars. "What shall it be?" It needed to be believable. Something, just a little off with the rest of the disguise. He'd learned a long time ago that matching expectations in every way would itself draw attention to him.

So, not too rough, not too deep. Something very different from his own. Ah, yes, that would do. He reached out and took one of the jars, unstoppered it, and put it to his lips. He inhaled the vapors and held his breath.

"That should do it." Yes, it should; that definitely wasn't his voice.

And the clothes. He wanted style—tasteful and elegant—but that wouldn't suit what he had in mind. Something from the provinces. Affluent but not ostentatious.

He closed the bookcase when he was finished. He opened the rosewood box and looked at the two phials. Each one was life for a day, more or less. What could he do with an extra day? Could he manage in three what he couldn't in two?

He couldn't do that to Caresa. He had forty-eight hours, less now, not more.

101

He took one of the phials and closed the box. Then he slid it into a pouch, and left the box and Caresa behind.

**Three hours since he had consumed the poison.**

Night had fully come as Maarkin walked along the bay, wanting to get further from his house before summoning a carriage. Once he was, he took the *orcinus* from his pouch and dipped it in the water. It made a series of chirps, and he settled back to wait.

*I've no time for waiting.*

It only took a few minutes for a carriage to approach. The waterman stood in the bow, illuminated by a lantern hanging from a pole. He reined the orca and lay out the gangway. "Where to, mate?"

"The *Arcada Piscus*, near the archival building, please." His new voice sounded strange to him.

The waterman shook his head. "Sorry, mate. I don't take fare to Wellspring District anymore."

"Why not?" Maarkin demanded.

"Makes me blackfish sick. Ain't a fish in the canals north o' Greenmarket."

"Is it as bad as all that?"

"The poor of Wellspring are starv'n on account o' not fishing any more. And eat'n the fish from the surrounding districts'll make ye sick 'cause the deathwater be gett'n worse."

"I'd heard that. Didn't know it was true, though."

"True 'nough. Hurts me too. I lose fare if I don't go to Wellspring, but what can I do?" He shrugged. "Can't make any money at all if me blackfish ain't healthy."

"Very well, can you take me to the Clearwater Plaza?"

The waterman smiled, his teeth white in the light of the lantern. "Sure thing, mate."

Maarkin crossed the gangplank and settled into the seat. "And fast, to make up for the walking I'll have to do."

"Aye." The waterman pulled in the plank and they were off.

The Clearwater Plaza still teemed with activity in spite of the hour. He'd forgotten it was five-night, and the market-barges were out.

They were called "coastermongers" and they sold their wares from barges. They were their own teamsters, fetching their goods and ferrying them about the city—a different plaza every evening,

102

bringing the market to the districts on a nightly basis.

Small boats jostled about the center of the plaza, vying for places to tie alongside the market-barges. A little of every smell imaginable assailed him. Bread and fish, land and sea. Coal smoke and ironmongery from the tinker's barge with its forge.

The waterman guided the carriage to the quay and threw out the gangplank. "A half-silver it is, mate."

Maarkin paid. The library was a long walk and locked door away. But it was better at night. He didn't want any nosey archivist looking over his shoulder. Nobody needed to know why he wanted to know if there were any limits on the Celestial Inquest's powers.

And, if he allowed himself a petty vanity, he could help himself faster than they could help him.

He hurried through the Clearwater District and into the Wellspring. Wellspring was the home of the Temple Complex, with the Temple Itself and all the supporting buildings—including its archives. Outside the Temple were the tenement houses of the working poor and a few of the holdings of the Duke of Savongy.

The archival building had many arches filled with convenient shadows. On some other night he might have wanted more of a challenge.

Not tonight.

He let himself in through one of the high windows in the reading room and paused on the ledge. The room had a certain beauty. The dim light from the windows highlighted the tops of the rows and rows of bookcases along the walls while leaving the rest in darkness. Lamps on the reading tables created a double row of light pools down the center of the room.

It appeared to be deserted and he didn't have time to waste. He dropped to the floor, listening.

"I would have let you in."

Maarkin froze. A man stood between two bookcases, just in the shadows, holding a book angled to catch what little light there was.

*Damn.* Maarkin hesitated, caught between fight and flight, cursing himself for the haste that made him sloppy. "You would have what?"

"Let you in. That seems a dangerous way to enter, but then you don't look like the sort who slips often."

"You might be surprised." The man didn't act alarmed. He went over to one of the reading tables where Maarkin could see him more clearly.

He was in his twenties, perhaps a touch older and wore clothes that were well-made and fashionable. He had money, maybe a title of nobility. He wasn't dressed in darkness, but compared to the flamboyant dress of other wealthy people... some might call it drab, but Maarkin would call it tasteful. He set the book onto the table with several others.

Maarkin said, "The library is closed."

"Is it? I wondered where the librarian had gone. Always hard to find one when you need them."

Maarkin glanced around, unsure if the man jested. They seemed to be alone. He could kill the man if needed.

"I'm Askel, by the way, *thalois* of Devenchy."

*Thalois* was the title of a second son. Devenchy... one of the Seaward Houses. They lived near Maarkin, in fact, in the Seawall District, the spit of land that protected the bay. He lived on the bayward side, their home was on the seaward side.

The Devenchys weren't well enough placed to avoid working, but because of that, they had become sorcerers and held commercial interests that made them wealthier than many Houses "too rich to work."

"Are you a sorcerer?" Maarkin asked.

"Not I," Askel said with a laugh. "My father handles most of the magic for the family, but my sister is quite the sorceress as well." They stared at each other for a moment. "Dare I ask why you're here?"

"Do you?"

Askel said, "You're either in a great hurry, or you don't want anybody to know what you seek. Or both."

"Have I asked you why you're here?"

"No. You have greater courtesy than I do. But I'll tell you anyway, I'm fascinated with the workings of the Temple. I'd join, but I like good food, being comfortable, and the company of pretty women."

"You're unlikely to meet any in the library at night," Maarkin said. "You might have better luck in the day. And the answer to your question is both. Not only don't I want anyone to know what I seek," he lowered his voice to make it sound ominous, "I don't want them knowing that I seek it."

"Oh, no need to worry. I don't *really* care why you're here. I'm here, well, I'm here because I gave so much money to the Temple that they gave me a key to the building. But what I want right *now*, is a clue to the deathwater."

"Admirable." Maarkin started to move away. He couldn't afford to waste time.

"The Duke of Savongy is using the deathwater for political reasons, which I don't care about, but he's using it to pressure my sister into marriage, which I do."

Maarkin paused. "How is the Duke using the deathwater?"

"We're a Seaward house, and the water is important to us. Savongy is using promises of cleaning the deathwater to gain favor among the Seaward houses. My father already looks favorably on his proposal to my sister Amber, and if Savongy can truly clean the canals, I think he would agree."

Anything dealing with Savongy interested Maarkin. "You don't approve?"

"Amber doesn't. She has an uncanny ability to read people and she does *not* like Savongy."

That was curious, given his shining reputation. Also curious was, "why does he need the favor of the Seaward houses?"

Askel shrugged. "I don't know. He has an important project he's been working on for some time—something too big for him to do alone. He has support from some of the Landward nobles and wants it from at least some of the Seaward ones."

"What is this project?"

"Very secret," Askel said with a laugh. "I don't know, but he'll complete it soon. He told father he'd be betrothed to Amber within days."

"So you're trying to find a way to clean the deathwater before Savongy does so your sister doesn't have to marry?" Was "days" two days? Maarkin wondered. It would look bad if Calex forbid Savongy from marrying Amber Devenchy, but that was nothing compared to being discovered involved in the assassination of a popular noble.

"I don't have much time because tomorrow evening Savongy is having a party and it's almost impossible to refuse the invitation of a Duke."

Maarkin said, "Almost as hard as refusing a king."

"Except one can't refuse a king. So far Amber's been able to refuse the Duke."

"More luck to her." Maarkin started to gather books about the Inquest. "If you don't mind, could you tell me more about Savongy?"

"If you want."

It wasn't prudent to give his own goals for Savongy, but Askel might inadvertently give him some useful information.

The two worked alongside each other, Askel cheerfully gossiping about the Duke of Savongy. He took delight in telling how superstitious the man could be. He was currently obsessed with the painter Mali whose paintings all contained some form of prophecy.

"He's going to buy the latest Mali in the morning," Askel said. "In some strange way it's tied to this project of his, as if the prophecy in the painting is directed at him."

Maarkin stopped reading. He actually knew Mali; she lived near him and sold her paintings through Bellagia's gallery. "Going to buy?"

"In the morning," Askel confirmed.

"You know a lot about his movements."

Askel frowned. "He likes my sister." He closed the book he was reading with disgust and went to find another, more helpful, one.

Maarkin turned his attention back to the Inquest.

The breadth of power the Inquestor wielded was daunting. The Celestial Inquest drew its power directly from the divinity, he learned. The Vicar General invoked the goddess, who would be present within her until the completion of the Inquest. With the goddess answering questions, the Inquest could be completed quickly—good news, he supposed, to beat the poison. Irrelevant if he couldn't beat the Inquest.

He closed the book and returned it to its place. Though it wasn't quite lauds, he thought again of the poison inside him. In him and in Caresa.

He let his hand stray to his pouch to reassure himself the phial was still there. Should he hide it to avoid breaking it?

Hiding things... *Of course.* He needed to hide the fact the Duke was dead. Nobody would convene the Inquest for somebody they thought still lived. Kill him, take his place.

It wasn't a perfect solution, in fact it was a bad idea, but if he could manage it for a day or two, he could arrange a trip, or bluster his way into... into something.

He might need to fake an illness on which to blame any slips of character. Something contagious to keep the servants at a distance...

But he needed to learn to mimic Savongy before killing him. He needed to observe the man.

106

**Ten hours since he had consumed the poison.**

Maarkin stopped at the end of the canal and looked toward Savongy's mansion. It wasn't as large as other mansions, but nobody would mistake it for anything else than the home of a powerful man. It harkened back to the inland fortresses, not surprising since his was one of the Landward houses. But gilded. Marble veneered the granite. Steel, burnished to mirror brilliance, accented the crenellated roofline. The house was everything one would expect from an old, powerful, wealthy Landward family.

Maarkin settled in to watch, praying Savongy would leave soon. He couldn't barge into the house and arouse everybody's suspicions. He'd learned his lesson—haste could ruin all his plans.

An old man sat huddled next to the canal, his ragged collar turned up against the chill of the morning. He held a fishing pole in his gnarled hands. The line led to a bobber made from a folded scrap of paper and disappeared into the murky water.

Surprised anybody would be fishing, Maarkin asked, "Any luck?"

The old man craned and turned his head to look. "'Course not. Hasn't been any fish in this canal for more'n a year."

"Why fish here then?" He reached into his pocket for a small coin. "You need the food that badly?"

"Not 'xactly, no. Duke gives out food from his farms. I just been fishing the canal my whole life. Been awhile since I had fish and I got a taste for it."

"The Duke... Savongy?"

"Sure 'nough. Comes through with food, he does. Took him a bit, folks was getting hungry, restless like. There was talk o' making trouble, or o' petitioning the king, but the Duke said no, he'd see us through 'cause he has holdings in the Wellspring."

After a moment of silence, the old man said, "Sitting here reminds me of the old days, even if the fish are gone."

Nobody profited from the deathwater, not the people who could no longer fish the canals, not the king who looked weak because he couldn't solve it. Not even Savongy, unless the good-will of the commons was worth the cost of feeding them. That was the gambit of kings though, not dukes.

*What will happen to these people if I kill Savongy?* He pushed aside the thought. *They can petition the king. It'll be his fault.* He pulled his hand from his pocket, still holding the coin. "Enjoy the day," he said, dropping the coin on the flagstone next to the man. "Then buy yourself a fish."

He moved away, wondering when the Duke would go to collect the Mali. Maybe he *should* sneak into the mansion. He needed to watch the way Savongy interacted with his servants; thankfully the man had no family.

*Patience. It wouldn't do to climb in a back window while Savongy walked out the front door.*

He couldn't shake the feeling that impersonating Savongy was a bad idea, that if he was half the assassin he used to be, he could do better.

*I can do better by making it work.*

And he could make it work by being patient and not making mistakes.

He didn't have long to wait. A carriage drawn by matching orcas came out of the mansion's private canal and turned into the main canal. The Duke sat under a light green awning, flanked by guards. He checked his pocket watch as they passed Maarkin.

"Belliaga's first, I think," he said to the driver. Savongy was a Landward house and it showed. Some people never learn how easily sound travels over calm water.

Maarkin waited until the carriage turned the corner before racing away. If he used enough short-cuts, he could arrive at the gallery not much later than Savongy.

He did, arriving in time to watch Savongy climb out of his carriage. Savongy let two guards enter the gallery, and entered himself with the last guards following. Maarkin waited a discrete moment and entered.

The owner, Belliaga, didn't even look at him. "Of course it's ready, My Lord," she said to Savongy. "I've had it re-framed and contacted Mali as you asked."

"And?"

Belliaga spread her hands in a gesture of 'I've tried, but what can I do?' "She claims to not know the prophecy of the picture. She would neither confirm nor deny the person pictured is you."

"Did you offer her money?" Savongy demanded.

"I did."

"And you made it clear I don't care about the truth, if she'll just say what I want?"

"My lord," Belliaga said warningly with a look at Maarkin across the shop.

Maarkin made himself busy looking at the artwork.

Belliaga spoke more quietly, but Maarkin could still hear her. "I did. She would not agree."

"You assured me this wouldn't be a problem." Savongy sounded angry. "I arranged a party *tonight* on the assumption Mali would be there."

Maarkin dared a glance over his shoulder to see Belliaga with a helpless expression on her face. "I did my best, My Lord, even promising to take lower commissions on future pieces. She said it is common knowledge she doesn't know the prophecies she paints, to pretend otherwise would ruin her reputation."

Savongy swore. "I am displeased." The gallery was silent, waiting for what he would do. "Show me the new frame," he commanded.

"Over here, My Lord."

Maarkin moved so he, too, could see the painting from across the gallery.

"I chose the dark interior with the gilded exterior because it mimics the dynamic imbalance of color Mali uses in the painting," Balliaga explained.

"Yes, yes," said Savongy impatiently. "But the true questions are, is this figure me, and if it is, does the painting forewarn me of a perilous future?"

*Mali, what did you paint?* Maarkin moved forward to see more clearly. On the right side of the painting a stylized figure stood on the edge of a canal. It could be anybody; it might be Savongy. It faced the Palace of Azure and Onyx, making further identification difficult.

The left side of the painting was full of shadows.

"Rather ominous, I should think," Belliaga said. "Were I sure it was you, I'd advise you to take caution. Look here, in the shadows to the left is another figure, *very* hard to see."

*Is that me? Oh no. Mali, if I didn't know you, I'd say you were trying to get me killed.* "Maybe," Maarkin burst out. He did not want Savongy warned; it would make his job harder. The two turned to give him a disapproving look and he was glad for his disguise. "That's one way to look at it," he said hastily. "But I think there are others."

He took a step closer, only to have Savongy's bodyguards move to cut him off. He raised an eyebrow and lifted his palms toward the goons. *Really?*

"Sir, I will not allow you to disturb my other patrons," Belliaga said.

"Let him talk," Savongy said. "You have some insight into this painting?" he asked, wiggling a finger to indicate the guards should let Maarkin closer.

"Mali is very hard to interpret," Maarkin said. "But not all her foreshadowings are bad. Everybody thought *The Diamond Fish* had a deep, diabolical meaning, but it was really just a boy finding a diamond in the stomach of a fish."

"Are you an expert?" Belliaga said with a sneer in her voice.

"I wouldn't claim that title, not in present company. I merely say there are other ways to view the work."

"I'm listening," Savongy said.

*He must really want to know the future,* Maarkin thought as he studied the picture. "The man—person, I assume it's man but with Mali one shouldn't assume anything—is facing the palace. He's distracted? Is he focused on approaching the palace, or is he looking back as he leaves? We don't know. It might not matter."

Belliaga snorted.

Maarkin ignored her. "As has been mentioned, this figure here..." He pointed to the man in the darkness.

"Which the first man is clearly unaware of," interjected Belliaga.

"That seems likely," Maarkin admitted.

"So it is logical that the man in the light should fear the man in the shadows. Why would he be in shadows other than to do harm?"

"Any number of reasons," Maarkin insisted. "As I said, one shouldn't assume with Mali."

"Then you're saying this isn't a warning for the man in the light?" Savongy asked.

*I mustn't overplay my hand. Just seed doubt, that's more credible than an outright denial.* "It might be. The clue, I think, is in the sky."

"The sky?" Savongy asked, surprised.

"There are shades of red in this portion, as we move from the light to the dark. It brings to mind the old sailor's weather saying—"

"Sailors take warning," said Belliaga with obvious triumph.

"Red sky in the morning, sailors take warning," Maarkin agreed. "But red sky at night? Sailors delight. The question is, is this a sunrise or a sunset?"

"So the figure in darkness might be harmful to m—to the man in the light," Savongy mused. "Or he might be helpful." He glanced

110

from the painting to Maarkin. "You seem to know your Mali."

"There is a certain... art to life. One tries to appreciate it." Maarkin tried to sound cavalier.

"Do you? Indeed. What is your name?"

"Gerard," Maarkin answered.

"Well, Mister Gerard, I have another Mali in my home. Nobody has given me a satisfactory interpretation. I'd like you to give me your opinion. Should it be—convincing—I might want you to share it with some friends of mine."

Elation filled Maarkin, but *I don't want to appear too eager.* "My opinion? I don't know if that's worth your trouble, but," he went on before the gallery owner could speak, "I'll give it my best try."

Belliaga sniffed.

"Then we shall go right now," Savongy said.

"Right now?" The demand surpassed any expectation. It was perfect chance to watch and learn Savongy's mannerisms.

"I have time now."

Belliaga made a small sound of distress.

Savongy gave her a glance. "I'll take this picture with me." He gestured to one of the guards. "Pay the woman." He didn't wait to see his order carried out. Beckoning to the door, he indicated that Maarkin should precede him. "Mister Gerard."

**Fifteen hours since he had consumed the poison.**

*M*aybe this is why I'm not a very good assassin.
Maarkin longed to "just get on with it." The movement of the carriage through the canal wasn't particularly slow, but it felt that way. He felt the press of time more acutely when Savongy checked his watch again.

*Haste will get me killed,* he reminded himself.

He watched Savongy's every move, every mannerism as they disembarked and noted every detail as they moved through the building. Savongy was unique, it would be difficult to mimic him.

He watched the house, noting the rooms, the furnishings. If he was to *be* Savongy, he needed to know the house.

"You have a remarkable interest in my house," Savongy observed.

"You have some remarkable art," Maarkin said.

"Ah. Yes. I do." He strode past a magnificent tapestry without a glance. "The Mali is down here."

They stopped at the end of a hallway, and Savongy drew back a curtain. "It disturbs the staff, so I allowed them to cover it."

Maarkin understood why. Even for Mali it was unusual. It resembled a nightmare. At first glance it was a man stumbling as he fell, looking over his shoulder at a man with a deformed face.

"That's odd," Maarkin said. "This man here, these scars on his face—two slashes. They are very distinctive." Savongy didn't react. "I'd love to be able to see the stumbling man's face. He's an old man, that's clear."

"How do you know?"

"Look at his hands."

Savongy leaned forward. "So. They. Are."

"The ground is uneven, that looks like a hole in front of him. He could be turning to talk to this man and stumbles. He could be startled by the man, or the man could be intentionally scaring him. Yes," Maarkin mused, "I'd love to be able to see his face."

"Others have said the hole resembles a grave," Savongy said. "But the man isn't me." It sounded like a revelation.

*Did you think it was?* Mali paintings often found their way to the subject of their foretelling, but that didn't always mean it was by ownership. *Do you think all Mali paintings are?*

"I don't pretend to understand the meaning," Maarkin said. "But this is an old man, and you're not old."

"That is sufficient." Savongy tapped his left hand on the palm of his right. "I'm having an artistic gathering this evening. I think my guests would benefit from your interpretation."

Maarkin pasted a look of surprise, not entirely feigned, onto his face. "It'd be an honor. Very kind, if I may say."

"I believe, my friend, that my guests, who can be superstitious men, would be re-assured to talk with you."

"I can't image why." *And I couldn't care less, as long as I can watch you and take your measure.* "But as I said, it's kind of you to invite me."

"Yes." Savongy started to turn away, then paused. "What is it you do, my friend?"

"I'm a wool factor."

"Ah, a Landward man. I'm glad to hear that. Yes, even better. I'll be opening doors at the three-quarter chime. There's no true meal, but I don't think you'll be disappointed in the fare." He started to turn away again, paused again. "Expect it to last four hours."

112

*Perfect.* He bowed his head in acquiescence.

Savongy turned away. This time he didn't stop.

**Seventeen hours since he had consumed the poison.**

Maarkin spent the day with watching. Watching Savongy when he could, and when he couldn't, he watched the household staff prepare for the party. And when three-quarter chime came, he presented himself at the front door. He was led to the garden and left to his own devices with a "the Duke will greet all his guests at his own convenience."

It gave him a chance to view the art that had been set up for the party.

All the greatest mansions had dolphin pens for their dolphins and orcas in addition to stables for their horses. They were connected to the public canal by their own, private waterway with ornamental gates.

Savongy's pen was just beyond the lawn, but in front of the stables. It was as gilded as the rest of his house. The large cement pool was stepped and tiled, the garden around it landscaped with rare flowers.

Magical light glowed in the pen, illuminating the crystal-clear water and the statuary inside. Several guests guided punts across the surface, viewing from all angles. There was a rack of towels, should somebody wish to swim amongst the artwork.

A high wall provided privacy and gave Maarkin a feeling of being transported outside the city. There were murals frescoed onto the wall and mosaics on the terrace. The small, verdant lawn was immaculate. Lanterns anticipated dusk, giving off the smell of sandlewood to mix with the roses.

Easels placed along the pathways held the non-immersible art while servants moved throughout with trays of crystal wine.

Maarkin was appreciating the way artistic way the light sparkled off the water over the statues when Savongy approached. "Mister Gerard," Savongy said, taking him by the elbow. "Over here. There are some important people who are interested in your view of the Malis." He guided Maarkin toward a group of nobles clustered around the two Mali paintings, now in matching, gilded frames.

A group of men had gathered around them. Some viewed the paintings while others stood waiting.

Savongy surveyed the group. "Where is Ardoit?"

One of the men scoffed, while others chuckled. "You didn't expect him to be *on time*, did you? Ardoit wants to hear what you have to say privately. He'll be as late as he needs to be to make it happen."

Savongy frowned. "A waste of time. Nonetheless," he went on briskly, "I shan't keep the rest of you waiting. There had been some talk of Mali and caution. It is unnecessary. I believe this gentleman can lay your concerns to rest."

Savongy introduced Maarkin as a "respected citizen of the land," whose observations "should be a refreshing change" for them. He didn't introduce the men, but Maarkin knew them to be powerful Landward men, none of whom shared Savongy's beneficent reputation.

He started at Savongy's original painting. "As you see—," he began.

"They all know what the painting looks like," Savongy said. "We've been talking about it for months. Tell them why they were wrong."

"Just the prophecy." *Why would this particular group of men care about Mali's prophecy?* Maarkin repeated what he told Savongy earlier and answered their questions.

All the while, he memorized Savongy's movements, the tiny motions he made when he wanted things to move more quickly, the signs of irritation he made when somebody questioned Maarkin's, and by extension his own, conclusions.

When Maarkin finished, Savongy said, "And that, gentlemen, is why we need not worry about any 'men in the shadows.'"

Maarkin listened as Savongy repeated what he'd said, emphasizing the uncertain nature of the prophecies. *Keep talking,* Maarkin thought. Tone, cadence, inflection: he needed to master them all.

But Savongy gave him brusque thanks and sent him off. He didn't dare argue, so he drifted away, took a goblet, and looked around for a moment.

He knew many of the people here, of course. Not just the nobles from his time at court under Jervis, but some of the artists from his neighborhood. Mali was not among them.

Nobody gave any indication of recognizing him.

He found a spot where he could watch Savongy and noted how he would tap his left hand on his right when he thought. He saw how Savongy consulted his pocket watch when events slowed down. That last was a bit of a habit.

A young woman walked across his vison. She looked up—happenstance, though assassins distrust happenstance—and met his gaze.

Her eyes caught the sun and held it, almost luminous. It took him a moment to realize her eyes were amber. Not light brown or golden-tan, but a rich orange-yellow.

*Your eyes!* He lifted his glass and sipped, both a salute and a way to cover his astonishment.

She gave him a wry smile, lifting her own glass. "I don't know you, sir."

"My name is Gerard; I'm a wool factor."

"No," she said. "You are not."

The wine went down the wrong way. Maarkin coughed. "What?"

But she didn't follow with another accusation. "I'm Dani Devenchy but I'm normally called Amber."

"Devenchy. What a coincidence. I know your brother."

"Which one?"

"Askel."

"The archival owl?" She laughed. "How did you meet him? You'll never find him in a crowd. Although," she said as she looked about the garden, "he's here somewhere."

She didn't seem bothered that he might not be what he claimed. Askel had said she was good at reading people so perhaps she didn't think him a threat—he wasn't, to her. But how could she tell?

He tried again. "If you say I'm not a wool factor, which I assure you I am, what do you think I am?"

She shrugged. "I'm sure I haven't a clue. I don't have second sight."

"Then what—why claim I'm not what I say?" His mind raced, afraid of what she might suspect.

"You know better than I do. You know what you are."

*I'm a damn poor assassin if I can be thrown off stride so easily. All it takes is an amber pair of eyes. And,* he added, *years of not actually being an assassin.* He shook his head. "I'm—" he stopped, unsure that whatever he might say would reveal about himself.

"All I know," Amber said, "is when something isn't as it seems. I don't know exactly what it is, just that it's not what it seems. A limited gift, but useful to the family business."

"That's not sorcery," Maarkin said, remembering Askel had also said she was a sorceress.

"No, it's not," she agreed.

"What is it? What are the limits?"

"I don't know what it is, and I don't know its limits. Sometimes it surprises me and I know more than just whether someone lies." She smiled.

He smiled in return. "It's a useful skill."

Her expression changed, turned hard and angry. "The Duke thinks it would be useful to him as well. He claims he likes me for my eyes. He thinks if he weds me he can use them, but he ought to be afraid."

"Afraid? Of what?"

A breath of breeze swirled through the garden, bringing with it the scent of her perfume. It smelled of coconut and citrus, and reminded him of the Seaward beaches.

"Nice of Savongy to invite you," she said as if he hadn't asked the question. "He's such a *good* man. Everybody agrees. He feeds the poor. Tithes to the Temple. Pays the artists. Does," she waved her hand, "whatever he did for you. Somebody should stick a knife in him."

"What?"

"He *ought* to be searching out the cause of the deathwater. A Seaward house would never neglect the water like he does."

A Seaward house... Devenchy *was* a Seaward house. He'd forgotten that. "What can you truly hold against him?"

"I don't know," she admitted, "but I know when things aren't what they seem."

"Then he and I are much alike, at least to your, if I may be so bold to say, remarkable eyes."

She smiled. "You are nothing alike."

*Because he is a good man, I am not, and bad men kill good ones.*

"And," she said with a sigh, "if somebody does stick a knife in our good Duke, a little light will go out in the Temple and the Inquest will see the intrepid hero slowly lowered into the shark pens as he's consumed from toes to head."

Her words were like cold fingers dancing on his back. "A light in the Temple? What are you talking about?"

"You don't think this sort of thing would be left to chance, do you? There are lamps in the Temple magically tied to the nobles' life. Should the noble die, the lamp will go out."

It felt like the cold fingers stopped dancing, reached inside his

116

back, and squeezed his heart. He couldn't keep Savongy's death from the Temple. Trying to take Savongy's place would not work.

"Are you alright?" Amber asked.

He forced himself to smile. "Yes, of course. That is clever, isn't it? The lamps, I mean." *Damn them!* "I wonder how they make it work."

"Blood magic, I'd guess, some secret spell of the Temple," she said.

Already he was rallying, trying to think, stalling the conversation as he wondered if the spell could be broken. He knew some blood magic; he might be soft, but he was still an assassin. He looked around, from guest to guest, seeking Askel, the man who knew so much of the Temple's workings.

He said, "If Askel's here, I ought to say hello. Please excuse me. He moved away as he looked for Askel Devenchy.

The poison's fire came quickly. It started in his fingers and toes, a warm tingling.

**Twenty-four hours since he had consumed the poison.**

The poison moved almost like a creature under his skin, creeping toward his wrists and ankles. He instinctively clenched his fist, shattering his goblet. Drops of crystal wine pattered across his shoes as the shards rained down.

He swept them under a bush with his foot and stepped away, almost fleeing to a secluded corner of the yard. He clenched and unclenched his hands. He wiped them on his jacket as if he could wipe the burning feeling away. Smother them, drown them, he couldn't keep still. He had to move his feet, his hands, as the burning intensified. Surely his skin was reddening, bubbling, charring!

He was sweating even though the feeling had just reached his wrists and ankles. He gritted his teeth, *goddess, this poison moves fast.* There was no way to wait four hours for the reprieve. He'd be dead in ten minutes if he tried.

He fumbled with his pouch, fingers twitching and shaking. He was afraid he couldn't do it, couldn't get the phial out, couldn't unstopper it, couldn't do anything but drop it.

It took all his concentration to wrap his hand around it and yank the stopper free. He cupped it in both hands to steady it and brought it to his lips. It clinked against his teeth as he desperately tried to hold it steady. He couldn't, so he took it between his teeth and let go. He tipped his head back and let the reprieve flow down his throat.

When there was no more, he dropped it into his hands and staggered to a nearby bench. There was a knot of coolness in his stomach that made him shiver as it crept outward. The cold met the heat at his elbows and knees and quenched it. Soon all that remained was a tingling in his fingertips and toes and even that faded.

The reprieve was gone.

He let out a sigh of relief nonetheless.

Goddess help Caresa if it happened to her too. He hoped she took the reprieve more quickly than he had. She surely had; she wasn't the kind to endure pain.

As much as he wanted to enjoy the luxury of being pain-free, he still needed to find Askel. In twenty-four hours the poison would kill him and he could not stretch it any further. He tucked the phial away and went searching.

He eventually found Askel in a quiet corner of the garden. He was alone drinking wine, and appeared surprised to see him.

"What a funny coincidence," Askel said. "I didn't even catch your name last night. Figured you wouldn't tell me the truth, and since I don't care, why ask?"

"Gerard," Maarkin answered. "My name is Gerard. I wondered if you could answer some questions for me."

Askel shrugged. "If I can. Get you a drink?"

Maarkin pinched the bridge of his nose, trying to clear his head. "No, thank you. You're something of an expert on the Temple."

Askel took a sip of wine. "If you mean, like a cross between an academic and a gawker, I suppose."

"What can you tell me about the Inquest lamps?"

He brightened, like a child asked to tell of his favorite game. "A *fascinating* use of magic."

*Not sure I like it*, Maarkin thought. "How does it work?"

"When the person tied to the lamp dies, the light goes out."

"Forgive me," Maarkin said. "I wasn't clear. I want to know *how* it works."

"Oh. Sorcerous link. The benefactor gives some blood to the Temple who uses it to link the person to the lamp. It's a one-way link, person to lamp, so when the person dies, the lamp does too."

"What if you extinguish the lamp?" Maarkin asked. *That would be easy.*

"Can't. Literally. It draws power from the person, so it'll burn underwater, burn without air, burn in spite of any anti-fire

118

enchantments you may cast on it. As long as the person lives, the lamp will burn, and not a moment longer."

"How many are there?" Maarkin needed to keep the conversation going as he thought.

"You could have checked last night."

"But I didn't."

Askel laughed. "Alright. Only six. The lamp is more a statement to potential murderers than actual protection. There are others the Temple would consecrate an Inquest for, but only six have made it a guarantee."

"Including the Duke of Savongy."

"Yes," Askel said, drawing the word out as he looked at Maarkin, giving the impression he was trying to divine the reason the Duke came up. "He's an odd one, though. The rest are known bastards. Getting a lamp is admitting somebody would want to kill you. Who would want to kill Savongy?"

Maarkin could think of several people, himself foremost. "How do you fool the lamps?"

Askel took a nervous drink of wine. "I'm not sure I like the way this conversation is turning."

"You're just chatting with a friend."

"Are you a friend?"

"Of the family." It was Amber who had spoken.

Maarkin and Askel turned in unison as she walked up. Maarkin raised an eyebrow. Why would she help him? Because he wasn't like Savongy?

"I know why you don't like Savongy," Askel said to Amber. "We know nothing about Mister Gerard."

"And that already ranks him more highly than the Duke. Besides," she cast an appraising glance at Maarkin, "there is something at the heart of him that reassures me."

"Fine," Askel relented. "It doesn't matter anyway. Whatever your intent, Mister Gerard, the information won't help you. You can't fool the Inquest. It is sanctioned by the goddess and the goddess will not condone a foul death."

Maarkin studied the siblings. He had fallen into trouble because he let himself grow rusty. He had wasted time on an unworkable plan because of it. He could not afford pushing too hard if it would cause either of them to alert Savongy.

Fortunately, Amber seemed to favor him, and Askel deferred to

119

her judgement. "But I thought the Inquestor ran the Inquest," he said.

"Maybe? The goddess will keep the Inquisition active until all involved are discovered. If that means nudging the Inquestor, well, she'll do it."

"You can't—guide their questions? Set things up in a way that they will follow wrong assumptions?"

"No."

"What if it's an accident," Maarkin protested. "Wouldn't they just be looking for something that wasn't there?"

Askel smiled. His reluctance fell away and he started to explain as if to a pupil. "It's really quite nuanced. Fascinating, truly. I could write a treatise about it."

"Maybe just tell the extract," Amber said.

If he was offended, Askel didn't show it. "Say a person's heart gives out. That might be quite natural, or it might be induced by some drug, or it might even be natural but provoked. A person tricking a sick man into over-exerting himself, huh?"

Maarkin had thought of all these possibilities.

"So the first question the Inquestor asks is *what killed the victim?*" Askel continued. "If it's something easy like 'a crossbow bolt through the eye,' she can get on with the who. If it's 'a raging fever,' then she needs to find out if the fever is natural or not." He shrugged. "Often the Inquest is short. What killed him? Time. Bang, end of Inquest. The goddess has no interest if somebody died of old age.

"But if it's odd..." Askel continued, he had forgotten his reservations of telling Maarkin, "what killed him? His heart gave out. But he was only twenty-three. Ah, why did his heart give out? You see?"

Maarkin nodded. "But what if it were natural *and* the victim were twenty-three?"

"Well, that would be natural. Unusual, but still natural. The inquisition would ask what killed him, and the answer would be time. Bang, end of Inquest."

Maarkin nodded. "It still seems," he said slowly as he tried to formulate a new plan, "it would be impossible to know intent. You gave the example of a heart attack. What if you don't know a person has a bad heart when you urge them to exert themselves?"

Askel smirked. "You still killed them, just not on purpose. You can't hide intent from the goddess any more than you hide

120

accomplices."

"Leaving you at the mercy of the judge," Amber added with a sardonic smile.

"Not me, of course," Maarkin joked. *There'd be no mercy for me.* "I only ask out of curiosity."

Amber's expression could only be called speculative.

*I need to see that spell,* Maarkin thought. The only straw left to grasp was the hope that he could break the spell and make the unworkable plan workable.

"At least I'm already in the Wellspring," he muttered.

"Excuse me?" Askel said.

"Nothing, just thinking. Thank you. For your time. I've taken too much of it already."

### Twenty-five hours since he had consumed the poison.

After breaking into Temple's inner sanctum to read the spell of the lamp, Maarkin went to look at the lamps themselves. The lamp transept was deserted. Only the night priest slowly circled the nave, murmuring his prayers. He passed the transept every five minutes to checked the lamps, giving Maarkin time to think.

The spell, it seemed, required only some blood from the person and a lamp. Because it was blood magic, the spellcaster needed their arcane bloodstone. Since bloodstones were attuned to their owners, no other one would do. The person on whom the spell was cast needed to complete the ritual—they needed to be the one to light the lamp.

Once complete, the spell was unbreakable. If Savongy died, the lamp would go out. There didn't seem to be any way to prevent it.

Maarkin stood in front of the lamp, essentially staring for he didn't have any ideas. It was an ostentatious lamp, very ornate, with a gold base and burner, and a ruby crystal font. There was still a bit of fluid in the bottom—that would be Savongy's blood, which was no longer needed. The shade was also ruby crystal, and the chimney clear glass.

*He certainly thinks a lot of his life.* That fit what Maarkin had seen of Savongy, he did think much of himself. It clashed with his reputation as someone who cared more for others.

*There* must *be a way.*

The man in the shadows of Mali's first painting looked too much like him to be a coincidence, while the man looking toward the palace had the cast of Savongy. Why should Savongy fear Maarkin if he weren't a threat?

The man in the second Mali had a scarred face; two slashes, one longer than the other like the hands of a clock.

*Think, Maarkin, think! You don't have much time.*

Time... Time. Time!

Time could kill Savongy and the goddess wouldn't care.

He didn't have much, for even if Savongy died immediately the Temple needed to start the Inquest, but he had an idea.

He needed some of Savongy's blood, a substitute for the lamp, and his bloodstone to cast the spell.

He took the empty phial from the reprieve and filled it with Savongy's blood. Next, he needed Savongy's watch.

*Still in the Wellspring.* There would still be guests at Savongy's party, but he needed to go back.

**Twenty-seven hours since he had consumed the poison.**

Musicians were playing when he returned to Savongy's mansion. The light from within the dolphin pen illuminated the back part of the garden, giving it an enchanted feel. The pen was another world peopled by stone naiads. The musicians played on the patio while some of the guests danced. Food had been brought out and placed on tables and mostly eaten.

There were fewer guests and the party had the feeling of being on its last legs. Soon, enough people would have left that all the remaining guests would gather their jackets and leave.

He didn't see Amber or Askel, but that didn't mean they weren't there.

He tapped a servant on the shoulder. "Where's the Duke?"

"On his own business."

"I don't doubt it. I'd like to see him about some of mine."

"He never neglects his guests."

Maarkin pointedly glanced around. The Duke was not in sight.

"He is with other guests."

*Odd how a servant will judge the guests.* "Very well." He picked up a glass of wine and made a show of sipping it.

If Savongy wasn't outside, he must be in. Maarkin wandered inside and, sure enough, just as he entered, Savongy was taking a nobleman by the elbow and guiding him up the stairs. "If you'd arrived on time," the duke was saying, "I wouldn't worry about who might overhear. But several people have come in uninvited and my reputation as a generous man prevents me from dealing with them as I'd like." Maarkin followed them, carefully quiet and certain he was not seen.

Once the two reached the upstairs hall, Savongy spoke. "Now we can talk more freely."

Maarkin stopped half-way up the stairs, out of sight of the men above.

"I am at your service," came the voice of the other man.

"All right then, let's not waste any time. I've looked, I don't know where the idiot went. But I assure you, the prophecy doesn't apply to me." That was Savongy. He sounded peevish.

"Yes, I'm sure. Several of the others said he made perfect sense. So pleased for you. You want assurances of my support? Very well, I assure you, if your barge arrives from this mine you claim, and you give me the gold you promised, I will support you."

"Why do you doubt me, Ardoit?" Savongy asked.

Maarkin held his breath, not wanting to miss a word.

"You've promised a great deal of gold to people," Ardoit answered, "and nobody knows if the mine is real."

"The same quicksilver that kills the fish refines my gold. Your gold. Yours and the other Landward nobles. In two days you shall be extraordinarily rich, I shall be king, and we shall make this a proper Landward country."

"I'm not opposing you, Savongy," Ardoit went on. "And when I get my gold, my men will march alongside yours."

*Goddess! The Seaward nobles won't stand for that!* Maarkin thought. *There will be civil war.*

"The others are not so reticent," Savongy muttered.

Maarkin decided it was time to act. "Duke?" he called. "My Lord Savongy?" He staggered up the last few stairs. "My Lord Savongy," he said, slurring his words. "I been looking for you. A great party. Best. Art. Ever."

Savongy drew himself up. "Mister Gerard. I was looking for you earlier. Where did you go?"

"Wandering a bit." He hiccupped. "Here and there." He held up his glass. "Great wine. Viewing all the art. You know, you have a woman with gold eyes here?"

"I am aware." Savongy turned to the nobleman next to him. "This is the man I was telling you about, the one about the Malis."

123

At the foot of the stairs, the servant Maarkin had questioned walked past. He looked up and saw Maarkin. "Hey! You're not allowed upstairs."

*Perfect.*

Maarkin started. "What?" He splashed his wine across Savongy's jacket. "Oh! Sorry. I'm sorry. I just wanted to thank you and say good night as I left." He tried to brush off the wine.

"You dolt!" Savongy exclaimed. He raised his hand to strike.

"Sorry." Maarkin took hold of the collar and started to wrestle the jacket off. "Here. Let me. Don't want the wine to soak through to your shirt. Here, man, come here," he called to the servant.

Savongy pulled away, partly pulling his jacket off, then gave in, angrily shedding it and leaving it hanging in Maarkin's hands.

"Here," Maarkin said, holding the coat out to the servant. "Take this to the Duke's chambers and bring him a fresh jacket."

The servant gingerly took the proffered jacket. He looked to Savongy for confirmation.

"Yes, yes," Savongy said. He glared at Maarkin. "You said you were leaving?"

"Yes, yes. So sorry." He backed away, half-bowing, purposefully comical until he reached the top of stairs. He felt his foot hit the air, then let out an exclamation and tumbled down. At the bottom he rose to his feet, still apologizing. He was rewarded by seeing Savongy's smug smile.

*He thinks I've gotten what I deserve,* Maarkin thought, *so he won't try to have me beaten.* Not that it was likely tonight. Savongy still needed his reputation. But why take chances? Maarkin knew how to fall down stairs without getting hurt.

He staggered away, slurring "leaving now" as he went. Once outside he let Savongy's watch slide out of his sleeve where he hid it. He tucked it into his own pocket and headed to the garden gate.

Now he needed his arcane bloodstone.

"What happened to you?"

He jumped. Amber laughed. "You startled me," he admitted. *Sloppy. Too focused on leaving.* He looked at himself, unsure what she meant. His clothes. They were disheveled from falling down the stairs. "I—ah," he looked into her amber eyes and decided not to lie. "I fell down the stairs."

"How clumsy."

"Not particularly." He straightened his jacket. "But I was just leaving." He bowed and smiled. "It was a true honor meeting you."

"You have a carriage?"

"I was about to summon one."

She smiled. "I'd be happy to give you a ride. Askel is going to the archives, so there's room in my carriage. Where do you live?" she asked.

"I don't want to trouble you," he said. She waved off his protest so he said, "Seawall."

"How convenient. We're there too. Seaside?" she asked.

"Bayside," he answered.

"We're a true Seaward house," Amber said. They stepped through the gate to where a half-dozen carriages lined Savongy's private canal. She gestured to a small, two-person carriage harnessed to a team of four dolphins. She leapt into it without waiting for the driver to put out the gangplank.

Not wanting to look clumsy or hesitant, Maarkin jumped after her. He waited for her to sit, but she didn't.

"Very good!" she exclaimed. "You were born on the water, I see." He wasn't about to tell her much of his agility came from the rooftops. "My father says our blood is part saltwater."

"Where to, Miss Amber?" asked the driver.

Amber glanced at Maarkin, and he said a landing near his house. She relayed it to the driver and added, "Quickly. We're too close to the deathwater for the dolphins."

"The water's good enough, my lady," he said. "They'd tell us if it weren't."

"All the same, *I* don't like this area of the city either."

Maarkin had never seen such well-trained dolphins. All four swam together, their tails moving in unison. It was surreal, the way they sashayed, and took him a moment to realize it must be a *game* to them.

Amber didn't even sway as they surged through the canals. It was nice, the speed. She smiled her appreciation that he didn't fall and called, "Faster," to the driver. It was a game to her too.

He found himself enjoying the speed. The sooner he retrieved his bloodstone, the sooner he could cast the spell.

They slowed as they entered the Seawall District and the canal became more crowded. It was the last rush of the day, when the late shops, the ones which competed with floating markets, closed.

**Twenty-nine hours since he had consumed the poison.**

Maarkin stood on the steps to his house, the water of the bay lapping mere feet behind him. The lights were on in the upstairs bedroom. Caresa was home.

There was no reason to disguise himself. Having a stranger enter the home would just confuse things. If his idea worked, they would both live and be free. If it didn't, there wasn't enough smoke in the world to confuse the Inquest.

He wiped the putty from his face as he slipped in the door. Up the steps into the main room and he stopped, noting two things that were out of place.

A case sat at the table, a wooden box with brass work; latch, hinges, and corners, and a leather handle. On the side was painted: *J Griff—Potions and Cures.*

From the bedroom came the sounds of sex.

Maarkin's anger carried him across the room and up the stairs. Caresa saw him in the doorway and screamed. A middle-aged man leapt from the bed, scrambling to get behind it. His eyes were wide with shock and fear.

Caresa was breathing heavily, her shock turning to anger. "What are you doing here?" she demanded.

"It's my house," he retorted. "Tell me he's not here for the reason I think he is."

"He can cure the poison."

"Is that true?" Maarkin demanded, though he knew it wasn't. He needed J Griff to say it.

Griff's mouth moved but no sound came out. His face was flushed and glistening with sweat. He leaned over, as if to use his ample stomach to conceal himself.

"Can you cure a new poison developed by Felkirk?" Maarkin repeated. Griff shrank back from his anger. *Maybe I'm not completely soft.*

Griff looked away. "No."

Caresa caught her breath.

"Were you ever going to tell her?" Maarkin asked.

Griff looked around, at anything but either of them. He didn't answer, which was answer enough.

Maarkin crossed the space between them, was on the man before he could move. He grabbed him by the neck and arm. Griff pulled back but Maarkin ducked under and behind, adding his pull to Griff's movement and propelling him out the window.

Griff's scream ended in a splash.

"Lucky bastard," Maarkin said with a growl. "Didn't think he'd clear the pavement."

"How dare you barge in here," Caresa shouted.

"Into my own house?" he shouted back. "What were you thinking?"

She stared at him, filled with righteous anger. Suddenly she crumpled and started to cry.

Maarkin snorted. He grabbed her robe from the back of a chair and threw it to her.

"He said he could cure me," she said. "I don't want to die."

"And this was your answer?"

"He said he could cure me!" she wailed. She leaned forward, ignoring the robe. "Did you *feel* the poison? My whole hand was tingling."

"I felt it," he said.

"Then why didn't you do something?"

"I'm trying," he retorted. "And this doesn't help!"

"Trying?" She started to laugh, hysterically. "Oh, goddess, I can't take this anymore." Her face was frozen in an anguished grin as tears streamed down her cheeks. "Just kill me!" she screamed. "What does it matter to you?"

"You're a fool. You're a damned fool."

"What was I supposed to do, you bastard? You left, and I'm supposed to just sit, not knowing if I'll live or die. I had to do something!"

Maarkin shook his head, trying to shake free of the anger. It wasn't working. "You thought that idiot could cure a royal poison?" He pointed out the window Griff had flown through. "I'm better at poisons than he is!"

"You never told me!"

"I did! You didn't believe me. I wanted to protect you from the Inquest. That was a mistake." In several ways, apparently.

"Protect me? You arrogant bastard!" She picked up a book from the nightstand and threw it at him. It hit the wall next to the window. She picked up a wine glass and threw it. She grabbed the arcane bloodstone.

"Wait!" Maarkin shouted.

She threw it. Badly. He jumped for it, but it passed just beyond his fingers. Out the window. Into the bay.

**Twenty-nine and a half hours since he had consumed the poison.**

He stood staring into the dark water of the bay. It was black, the waves edged in reflected light from the lights behind him. The water was, rather ironically, twice six feet deep—twice the depth of a grave, or maybe the depth of two graves. The bloodstone lay somewhere among the rocks, maybe close, maybe not, depending how the current caught it as it sank.

It wasn't possible to use another mage's bloodstone, nor could he attune a new one to himself. That took a full lunar cycle.

What else could he do but dive to try and fetch it? Marking time until he died, as it were, for there was no hope he could find it.

He wouldn't go back inside. He had nothing to say.

*I can't cast the spell, and that ends my hopes.*

He couldn't cast the spell, but would another? Amber Devenchy, in addition to her strange power to tell truth from falsehood, was a sorceress. Could she cast the spell? Could she was the first question, would she was the real one.

He hated to ask. If his plan didn't work, she would go to the shark tank.

He would ask.

The Devenchy mansion was a twenty-minute walk, and the servant who opened the door made no comment about the lateness of the day. He merely said, "I shall inquire if the lady is available," and left to do so.

A few minutes later Amber entered. She stopped when she saw him. "You are not Gerard."

"I am," he said. "You said I was not what I seemed, and you were right. My name is Maarkin, and this is my true face."

She did not argue, just looked at him.

"I am an assassin."

"No," she said. "You are not."

He blinked in surprise.

"I've never read anybody so strongly," she said. "You're angry, and hurt, and..." her voice took on a note of wonder, "dying." She shook her head as if to clear it and looked at him again. "You're

128

dying."

"I thought you could only tell when things aren't what they seem."

"I—that's—yes, but the power is unknown... and there is something... it seems... I don't know." She walked to the window, barely glanced at it. "Why are you dying?" she burst out.

"I'd rather not say."

"Then why are you here?"

"To ask too much of you. Have you an arcane bloodstone?"

"You want a spell," she said. "I have one, but bloodspells are spells of binding and killing. They do not heal."

"Nor cure," he said a little sharply. "Sorry. I know. Whatever your gift says, at the moment I am an assassin, and I need a spell cast. I recently," a bitter laugh escaped him, "lost my own bloodstone."

"Which spell?"

He looked away. "If it doesn't work—"

"My spells usually do."

"If your casting doesn't work, there is no harm. But if your casting works, and my plan doesn't, you will die."

She drew in her breath. "Why would I agree to that?" She looked at him suspiciously. "What is your plan?"

"To kill the Duke of Savongy."

"Oh goddess. You're asking me to kill someone. And the Duke—he's protected by the Inquest."

He looked away, looked back, caught her golden eyes and let her see his honesty. "I think I can beat the Inquest."

"That's why, I need to remember you're Gerard. That's why you were asking about the Inquest."

He nodded. "I think I can beat the Inquest, but I can't cast the spell because I lost my bloodstone."

"What if I say no?"

"I won't do anything to draw you in. There will be no Inquest that discovers you had knowledge of the plot."

"You would die? And would Savongy live?"

"And become king," Maarkin admitted. "And the deathwater grows worse."

"What?"

He explained all he knew of Savongy's secret mine, the deathwater, and the plot to buy support of the Landward nobles. "The day after tomorrow a barge of gold will allow Savongy to launch a coup against the king."

"You're telling the truth, I can *see* that," she said. "Could he really overthrow the king?"

Maarkin shrugged. "Perhaps, yes. Calex hasn't established himself yet. If Savongy can buy the most powerful Landward houses and even a few of the Seaward ones... there would be fighting, but he's prepared for it."

"He pretends to be a good man, but he's not, and he'd be a bad king." Her tone hardened. "But he's protected by the Inquest. Nobody beats that."

"I stole a spell from the Temple, I think it will work."

"Blood magic requires some of his blood," she said.

"I have some."

She didn't say anything, but looked as though she pondered his proposal.

*I'm lucky she's even considering it*, he thought. *I'm asking too much.* He almost hoped she'd say no.

"This is some favor you do me."

He flushed, realizing he hadn't offered payment. "I'm sorry. I don't mean to try to take advantage of you. Anything I have is yours as payment."

She turned away. "If I had any doubt that you're dying, that settled them."

*Damnation. She doesn't deserve this.* Goddess knows he didn't owe the king his throne. Caresa might not deserve death, but at the moment he couldn't believe he owed her anything either.

On the other hand, he might be feeling low, but he didn't want to die. And he hated the idea of Savongy getting his way.

Amber drew his attention back. "But I meant it when I said you do me a favor, because you forgot something on your list."

"What's that?"

"Savongy becomes king, the deathwater becomes worse, and I get married."

"You get married?"

"It's impossible to decline a proposal from the king. He'd be a bad king, but a worse husband. I am not going to let that happen."

Maarkin showed her the blood and the watch. "It's mostly the same spell as creates the vigil lamps."

She picked up the watch. "You want to tie his watch to his life so he never has to wind it?"

"No, I want to tie his life to his watch so he ages a year with every second."

Her eyes widened as she understood. "Killed by time. That's clever."

"It's my hope the Inquest won't investigate somebody who died of old age."

"Askel said they don't, but will this," she faltered, uncertainly in her golden eyes, "qualify?"

"I—I don't know for sure. You don't have to help," he said.

"Yes, I do. For both of us. How long do you have?"

He shrugged. "Fourteen hours."

"I'll get my bloodstone."

**Thirty hours since he had consumed the poison.**

It was easy to sneak into Savongy's house. There were guards, but he avoided them. There were locks, but he picked them. There was absolute silence where the smallest noise would sound like thundering giants, but he made no noise.

He set the watch on the writing desk he found in Savongy's outer chambers—clearly the wrong spot but where a servant might lay it if they didn't know where it belonged.

He then withdrew, settling on the top of the roof of the mansion opposite with a pair of binoculars.

Savongy was an early riser. A servant entered the chamber, disappeared into the inner chamber. Several minutes later—an eternity to Maarkin—the man returned, followed by Savongy in a dressing gown.

The servant brought out clothes while Savongy questioned him. Maarkin couldn't hear their words, but after a moment the Duke went over to his desk and picked up some papers. The watch caught his eye and he picked it up.

Amber had wondered how Maarkin would get Savongy to complete the spell. "You can't light a watch like a lamp, and you can't just ask him," she had said.

"No," he had answered as he took the back off the watch and released all the tension in the mainspring, "but you can wind it."

Across the canal, Savongy tapped the watch and held it to his ear.

*It needs to be wound. Wind the watch.*

And he did.

The seconds ticked by. Savongy stared at his hands. His face transfigured with horror. He dropped the watch and rushed to a mirror.

The servant came over, stopped, and backed away.

Savongy staggered, his shoulders stooped, his skin wrinkled, blotches showed on his hands. He fell.

In the Temple, Maarkin was sure, his lamp went out.

Maarkin tucked the binoculars away and slid off the roof. He wanted to feel relief, and he did a little. The spell had worked, but would it fool the Inquest? And would the Inquest even be consecrated in time?

He raced to the Palace.

**Thirty-seven hours since he had consumed the poison.**

Maarkin was tired, angry, and in no mood for delays. "Where is the king?" he demanded of the royal steward.

"Last time you had an attractive companion," the man said. "Where is she?"

"Mine's the better question," Maarkin said. "Take me to the king." He assumed Caresa was still at his house. He hadn't had the stomach to check. He was tired—tired in a way he'd never been before. *Doesn't matter if I've gone soft now. That was my last kill. I wonder if it killed me too.*

"We don't normally demand things above our station."

Maarkin ground his teeth. "You know who I am and what I do. And if you don't know the king has business with me, you can ask him." He indulged himself by frowning. "It isn't wise to bait an assassin, especially one that needs to practice."

The man gathered his dignity by pretending Maarkin hadn't spoken. "If you will follow me," he said nonetheless.

Calex rose when they entered. "You bring me news?"

"Savongy is dead," Maarkin said.

The steward drew in his breath in surprise. Maarkin shot him a quick glare.

"Truly?" Calex gestured to the steward. "Go to the Temple, if they are not already consecrating the Inquest into Savongy's death, command them to do so."

He looked over at Maarkin. "Were you afraid I'd renege?"

"I thought it possible."

"It's not a bad idea, and I wouldn't even be breaking my word. All I need do is delay the Inquest until after you died from the poison."

Maarkin refused to be baited. He had already played his last card. He was too tired to do more than see out the hand.

"I'm not a nice man," Calex said. "But I keep my bargains."

Maarkin again did not respond.

"Your silence wasn't one of my conditions," Calex said.

Maarkin gave him a puzzled look.

"Should your plan work, we should bargain for your silence. I am prepared to pay handsomely for it."

*Is he trying to... redeem himself?*

"We'll go to the Temple. This concerns us both. My position as king isn't strong enough—it would not have been tolerated if I had as popular and powerful a man as Savongy killed without evidence. Even arresting him would weaken my already precarious position."

"You have no...?"

"Evidence," Calex said. "No. I know he plots—plotted—and that his plans matured tomorrow, but that is all. Was my information wrong?"

"No. It wasn't wrong."

Calex nodded. "Where's your lady? This concerns her too."

"She is... not here. This has strained her."

"Has it?" Calex glanced at him shrewdly. "Well, then, shall we go?"

*Too much time running around,* Maarkin thought, *but it must be done.*

**Thirty-nine hours since he had consumed the poison.**

Maarkin and Calex sat in the royal seats, an elevated box on the left of the nave which had its own entrance. People crowded the front of the nave while more and more kept filing in.

*How long until they start? This is taking too long.* He was aware of the angle of sunlight as the morning wore on. They had been sitting for hours, and he was beginning to worry.

The goddess-statue stood in the apse, just behind the high altar. Savongy's lamp rested on the high altar—extinguished. The Priestess stood to the right in her vestments. The vicar general stood before the altar wearing the robes of Justice—blood-red and trimmed in white.

"A great many Landward nobles here," Calex murmured. "Some of

133

them are still hoping for a Landward government if they can blame Savongy's death on me."

*Start the Inquest,* Maarkin thought. He had time before the reprieve wore off, but he wouldn't get the cure until the Inquest was over—if he would get the cure at all.

Calex must have read his expression. "If this doesn't work, the poison will be preferable to the sharks."

"How long does the Inquest last?" he asked.

"You better hope not long."

*That goes without saying.*

Two novices scurried down the aisle carrying clay jars. They paused to make obeisances, then took their burdens to the altar. Once they placed the jars, the vicar general stepped up and began the ritual.

*Finally.*

Earth and water—Landward and Seaward—in equal measures. The tooth of a shark for the punishment of the guilty. A font of the most pure holy water.

There was an invocation muttered under her breath, a few bars of a hymn hummed quietly and the eyes of the statue began to glow.

The vicar general placed her hands on the shoulders of the statue and leaned close. She inhaled deeply, drawing a glowing mist from the statue's eyes and into her mouth. Her eyes started to glow.

"Who has died?" she spoke, her voice fuller and richer than before.

"The Duke of Savongy," she replied to herself, her tones normal.

"Very well, ask me questions."

The vicar general stood up a little straighter. "What killed the Duke of Savongy?"

Maarkin leaned forward.

"Old age."

Murmurs of disbelief ran through the crowd. Calex glanced over at Maarkin. Both men were holding their breath.

"He was forty-one," protested the vicar general. "Yet he looked ninety when he died and kept aging even afterward."

"He died of the effects of time," the goddess voice said. "I have no interest in questioning the life of humanity."

Maarkin leaned forward.

"There must have—," the vicar general started.

She interrupted herself with the goddess voice. "I do not bother time, and he does not bother me."

The glow in her eyes faded as the goddess left.

The Landward nobles looked stunned.

Maarkin realized he was still holding his breath. He let it out slowly. *They said it wasn't possible, but I beat the Inquest.* He started to smile. *I beat the Inquest!*

"Smiling may not be appropriate here," Calex murmured. "Try to look like you expected this outcome."

"Smiling means I live." Nonetheless, he composed his face.

"Let's go back to the palace. Let them think about what they just witnessed. You need a cure."

#### Forty-two hours since he had consumed the poison.

Back at the palace, the steward brought Maarkin a phial filled with a thick, green liquid. He held it out, an offering. "Yours, Sir." He had been very polite since the Inquest.

"Felkirk died to keep this a secret," Maarkin said holding up the cure to examine before drinking.

"No, Felkirk's death was an accident," Calex said. "I misled you." He shrugged. "Two days ago, who would you have thought would make a better king, Savongy or me?"

Maarkin didn't answer.

"If I told you I didn't have a complete picture of what he planned, only that I had some of the pieces and no time to find the rest of the puzzle, would you have called it enough to justify killing him?"

Still Maarkin didn't answer.

"Had I not forced you, would you have even tried to kill Savongy?"

"No, probably not," Maarkin admitted reluctantly.

"I won't ask your feelings now. I don't care. But knowing that, and considering the chances that Savongy had already enlisted your help, I needed a lever long enough to force you to do my bidding. I couldn't be sure of anything less."

Maarkin wasn't sure either, and that confirmed he could no longer be an assassin. Assassins need black and white worlds. He drank the cure.

They waited until Caresa was brought to the throne room. She followed the steward, head down, shoulders slumped. She glanced from side to side. Maarkin wondered how much she knew of the day's events.

Calex spoke. "The Duke of Savongy is dead."

Caresa twitched. She swallowed and nodded.

"The Inquest has been held."

She finally looked up, eager and fearful.

"Here is your cure." Calex held out a phial of thick green liquid.

Caresa clutched her hands. With stiff, jerky motions, she lifted her arms and walked forward. When she was a step away she pounced, grabbing the phial like a hawk does a hare.

She tore the stopper from the top and lifted the phial to her lips. Half the phial disappeared into her mouth as she gulped. When she finished, her arms fell to her sides and she sank to her knees. The empty phial rolled from her listless hand. She let out a tremendous sigh.

"Yes," Calex said, "I imagine that's a relief. Now," he turned to Maarkin, "what deal shall she have?"

"Ask her," Maarkin replied. "She can't have what she wants from me."

"And what is it you want?" Calex asked Caresa. She stared at him with a blank expression. "A place to live?" She nodded once.

"I'll arrange a place for you in the Eastport District with enough money for furnishings. In return you'll never speak of what happened these last two days. Do you agree?"

*What choice does she have?* Maarkin wondered. It seemed generous though, and well chosen. He wasn't likely to see her often if she lived in the Eastport.

Caresa nodded. She rose and faced Maarkin. "You took the cure already?"

He nodded.

"Bastard. I nearly died because of you."

She was right, in a way, but not any way that would mend things between them. "You're leaving with more than you came with," he said.

She gave a little sniff and curtsied to Calex. "Your Majesty." He nodded permission for her to leave.

She gathered her dignity and her skirts and, back straight, nose up, left the room.

"I'm not sorry," Calex said. "She wore you like an ornament. You would do better with someone who sees you for who you are."

Maarkin nodded. "It's too soon for that, but perhaps."

"And now for you, what will it take to keep you silent?"

136

"Never ask me to kill for you again."

Calex laughed. "That's not even a request. Who would cross me now? *Savongy is dead.* All those who plotted with him know *the Celestial Inquest didn't save him or catch his killer!* You've bought me more than enough time to consolidate my position." He waved his hand. "Ask again."

"Savongy held land in the mountains along the Lifeblood river. I'd like it given over to House Devenchy."

"House Devenchy?"

"They will ensure the deathwater is cleaned."

Calex stared a moment before letting out a bark of laughter. "Savongy, that bastard! He caused the deathwater while bemoaning my 'weakness' in not solving it!" He shook his head. "But you can fix the deathwater?"

"Amber Devenchy can." Of that he had no doubts.

"What does she get in return?"

"A valuable holding." Which it was, even with the gold mines shut down.

Calex waved his hand again. "Again, that's not a request. I gain, Devenchy gains, and you can blab to anybody you want. I repeat, what do you want to keep quiet?"

"Well, since, I'm no longer an assassin, I'll need some way to pay my bills. Savongy has a barge arriving in the morning. Give it to me so I may dispose of the cargo as I wish and sell the vessel."

"Will that be enough?"

Thinking of how much gold it took to bribe already wealthy men, Maarkin said, "I'll manage."